Domestic Seduction

Domestic Seduction

Ann Keeys

PWP Romance

Passionate Writer Publishing

Indiana and Georgia

PWP Romance

Passionate Writer Publishing

www.passionatewriterpublishing.com

This book is a work of fiction. Names, characters, places, and incidents either are products of the author's imagination or are used fictitiously. Any resemblance to actual events or locales or persons, living or dead, is entirely coincidental.

978-0-9856125-7-3

First Edition

10 9 8 7 6 5 4 3 2 1

Manufactured in the United States of America.

Passionate Writer Publishing can bring authors to your live event. For more information or to book an event, contact Passionate Writer Publishing at www.passionatewriterpublishing.com.

Dedication

To all those in my inner circle, thank you for that extra push. I couldn't do it without you.

Other Mystery/Suspense Books by PWP

Unforgivable~Lisa Wooten
Fingerprints~Marcia Leonard

****

Dear Reader,

Thank you for allowing me to bring Vincent Hunter and Samantha Walker into your lives. I've written many characters but these two have been my favorite thus far. I love them so much that their story is also a script and currently being looked at for a movie adaptation.

I'd also like to mention that Reynoldstown did have an actual serial killer in the 90's. There are many rumors and unresolved issues regarding the real case and this is why I chose to highlight it again with my up to date spin.

Once again, thank you.

Sincerely,
Ann Keeys

Chapter 1

Vincent Hunter turned off the main monitor of the security system. Images of a foot with a butterfly tattoo on the ankle and purple diamond studded stiletto sticking out a dumpster were forever branded in his brain.

He drew a deep breath into his wide frame, developed from years of lifting weights, and headed into the hallway. The walk seemed more of the green mile than one to the head office. He stepped forward and the hall stretched forward before him. He had to let his boss know. Trepidation set in and images from 2008 pushed into the forefront.

A young detective tossed a case file onto Vincent's desk, interrupting him from completing the paperwork on his last case. "We got him."

Vincent leans back in his chair, his stone face unmoved, a stark contrast to the smiling disposition of the man standing at his desk. "Him who?"

"Mr. X, otherwise known as Mitchell Harold."

Hearing about his old partner's case captured his attention. Vincent flipped the file open and scanned the entries. Mitchell Harold had been in and out the system dating back to the 80's for robberies. His release coincided with some of Mr. X's murders. Mr. X's killing spree started in the early 90's. Mitchell Harold found himself back in jail for attempted rape in the late 90's. Time served, one year and four months. 2003 arrest for aggravated assault, only served a few months.

"Hold on. This shows his DNA was drawn in 2005."He flipped through the rest of the file and found no reason why the DNA had been drawn.

"So?" The guy shrugged, his enthusiasm slipping away.

"It's been three years. If his DNA was a match to a serial killer, then why the delay?" He shook his head and reread the arrest record.

"Who cares? This scumbag is off the streets. If he did or didn't commit the murders, at least he's not around to do any more harm. Besides, they were only prostitutes. No one cares about them." He walked off.

The attitude regarding the murders happening in a low income neighborhood and the victims being prostitutes unnerved Vincent. Unfortunately, it wasn't the first time he'd heard it. He refrained from expressing his distain and went back to his current case.

Vincent pressed the black buzzer and waited for the soft click to enter. "Boss lady, you have a second?"

He'd gladly worked for Erica as head of her security for the past year without incident and now the first issue is one he wouldn't wish on anyone. He'd just seen Amber's smiling face days before as she flirted with clients.

Green eyes peered at him from above a wide screen laptop. As usual she was hard at work insuring her business ran smoothly. Erica owned the number one adult club in Atlanta and poured her soul into keeping it that way. "Yes."

"Amber's…" As a former cop, he'd hardened against the brutality of the world. His employer, Erica was tough, but was she tough enough to handle this news? He'd soon find out. "Dead."

"Excuse me?"

"Amber is dead." He kept his gaze trained on her.

Her mouth gaped open. Manicured pink tipped fingernails flew to her mouth and covered it. Her eyes widened in disbelief. "How? When?"

"I'm not sure of the exact details, but I know for a fact it's her. We have a problem. This makes the second girl from your club. There's no way this is a coincidence. I can only protect them from the perverts inside these walls." He ran a hand through his thick dark tendrils. "This is personal. You need to contact APD immediately. I have someone in mind who will be great undercover."

"Whoa. What are you saying?"

He leaned in, ensuring she would fully comprehend his next words. "This is only the beginning."

"How do you know?"

"The killer left a message. One I know all too well." Along with the image of Amber burned in his brain was that of the message written in blood left on the ground. *I'm back, Mr. X and a smiley face.*

Her mouth gaped open. Yes, she understood.

Months after Mitchell Harold was convicted for the murder of one prostitute due to DNA evidence, Vincent shows up at a crime scene in the Reynoldstown neighborhood, located on Atlanta's east side.

"What do we have?" Vincent glanced down at the half naked girl's body then back up to the medical examiner. Seeing a young girl working as a prostitute bothered him. A dead one made it worse. Her left off-brand stiletto lay in the grass a few feet away.

"She was strangled, after being sodomized." The ME wipes away sweat from her forehead with the back of her elbow. "Poor girl. She can't be older than sixteen."

On the ground, written in blood a message, "Love, Mr. X.," followed by a smiley face.

Vincent swallows hard as his vision blurs.

Sam's car rolled to a stop in front of the local corner store. Her focus was on getting her favorite drink and energy boost before starting her shift.

"Are you coming home or not?" A voice filled with attitude spilled through Sam's blue tooth.

"I'm not sure yet, Tracey."

"What do you mean, you aren't sure?"

Her older sister Tracey had lived in Bowling Green, Kentucky, the same city as their parents all of her life while Sam moved far away as she could after graduating high school. Too bad it didn't get her very far—only an hour or so away. Sam was only able to get only so far with her full ride athletic scholarship for basketball. She landed at Tennessee State University. Once she graduated, she moved on to Atlanta.

Sam exited her car and took note of a group of neighborhood boys hanging out on the corner. They passed something between them and froze when she looked directly at them—guilt written all over their face. She continued toward her destination in hopes it was just a black and mild the teens normally smoked. Her wearing a uniform instantly made everyone around her act as suspects. The neighborhood wasn't the most trusting of the police.

"I'm not sure if I have to work or not—" Movement on the corner caught her attention, a plastic bag of substance exchanging hands. This time she saw it clearly. She whipped her head in their direction, and the dealer, took off in a sprint. "Don't you run from me! Dammit, stop. Don't make me chase you!"

"Sam! What's going on? What's all that noise?"

"Hold on a sec." She took off after him.

Sam followed the young male down the alley. She didn't have far to go. The sagging pants he wore made it difficult for him to move fast. Kids these days will never learn. She lunged and tackled him to the ground.

"I told you not to make me chase you. I was only going in the store for a drink, and you had to take off running. What are you running, Chris? You have some drugs on you again?" She put her knee in his back and yanked his arms behind to cuff him.

He tilted his head to the side, scrapping against the pavement. "Walker, man, let me up. I ain't done nothing. This is harassment."

"Harassment? Did you learn that up in county your last visit there?"

"You hurting me," he groaned.

"Well, you shouldn't have ran. I imagine it would hurt to be tackled on concrete. You have anything sharp or something I need to know about on your possession?"

He didn't answer. His lack of cooperation didn't stop her from patting him down. Chris's stash turned up in his left sock.

"Pills?" She tossed the lunch-sized bag of controlled substance to the side. "Wow, you've upgraded. You didn't learn from selling weed and being busted. You had to step it up? Three strikes and you're done for, kid. What a waste." She clicked on her walkie. "One male for pick-up. Two hundred block on Peachtree. Corner store."

"Sam! Sam!" A shrill voice screamed in her ear.

She'd forgotten all about the conversation.

"Yes, I'm back," she answered while keeping one hand on the cuffs and dragging Chris to the curb. He could sit there while waiting on transport.

"Tell me you didn't just arrest someone while on the phone with me?"

"Technically, I told you to hold on, so no." She gave Chris the eye. If he even flinched, she'd have no problem making him eat the pavement again.

"I thought you said you had just got on duty. Don't you think you take your job a little too seriously?"

Of course she took it seriously. Not taking it seriously could cost a cop their life.

"What does me just getting on duty have to do with anything? The boy had drugs on him."

"You didn't know it until you ran him down. You seriously need a partner."

Sam rolled her eyes. "I haven't had a partner in two years. Doubt I'll get one anytime soon. We barely have enough officers to patrol the beat as it is. Pairing us up would lessen our coverage."

"Anyway…" Tracey sucked her teeth. "Are you coming home for mom and dad's anniversary or what?"

Sam preferred the "or what" part, but she saw the paddy wagon turning the corner. "Hey, Tracey, I have to go. I have to talk to the transport guys." Perfect timing to evade the question.

She ended the call without waiting for an answer. The tan vehicle pulled up behind her squad car. Sam was one of the lucky few to have a new Charger.

"Corporal Walker, I see we're picking up one of your regulars." A tall brown-haired male closed the door on the passenger side and walked over to her. His name was Officer McClure. She typically saw him and his partner, Officer Jones, a few times during the evening.

"Yep, and we won't be seeing him around for a few years after this one. Third Strike." She despised adding more black youth to the system, but if they insisted on doing the crime, she'd keep ensuring they did their time.

"Tough break, but it's the same thing every day," Officer McClure responded.

He helped Chris up by grabbing him from behind—one hand on the top of Chris's shirt and the other on the handcuffs. The stubby fingers of Officer Jones waved at Sam as he walked to the back of the paddy wagon and opened the doors. They loaded Chris up and hauled him away.

The night was young. More kids from the neighborhood would undoubtedly join him. She didn't stick around for the door to close.

As she walked inside the gas station, her thoughts turned to how the neighborhood used to be when she had come to visit while in college. At one time, it had been a very nice area. A lot of older couples and people took pride in keeping up with their lawns. Years later, it seemed as if no one cared. Trash lined the streets, and broken bottles littered driveways.

"Officer Walker, you come for your usual?" Ameyn, the store clerk, asked.

"You know me. I have to have my Mountain Dew." She headed straight to the rear of the store where the coolers were. After grabbing two bottles, she turned and saw Ameyn staring at the nineteen-inch television. The old metal TV stand threatened to fall at any moment, duct tape wrapped around the legs for a last ditch effort to hold it in place.

"What you looking at?" she asked, walking up to the counter.

His gaze didn't move from the news channel. "They found another body."

"What else is new?"

He shook his head. "Another stripper girl found dead. The third one. She looks very young. I think it's a serial killer."

"Yeah, it doesn't take much to come up with that one." She looked at the screen.

Nineteen-year-old Jasmine Fuller's body was found in a dumpster behind a well-known strip club at six pm. No details on the cause of death but speculation leads to strangulation.

"Detective Hastings, do you think this is the work of a serial killer?" the reporter asked, shoving her microphone in his face as the cameraman zoomed in.

"What happened here is very unfortunate. Now, if you will excuse me." He stormed away from the reporter.

Sam took her eyes of the monitor. "Hastings wouldn't admit to it if he did have the coroner's report."

"Sounds like you know the guy," Ameyn said.

"You can say that. My concern is with those poor girls."

Hastings was a piece of work and her ex who couldn't keep his man below to himself.

She shook her head at another senseless death and handed her money to Ameyn. As usual, he waved her off, but she still paid anyway.

It was bad enough people were killing each other over small spats weekly, but a serial killer? This was something different all together. The only other one she'd heard of was in the 90's and that was debatable.

Back then, Reynoldstown's crime rate tipped the scales. The guy arrested for a killing spree was only convicted for one murder as she recalled. The case flew under the radar so much so that it was more of urban legend by the time she'd joined the force. This new serial killer would put the entire county in a state of unrest. Murders in the downtown area would be deemed too close to home. There were merely blocks separating the rich from the poor.

"Later." She made her way back outside and headed to her squad car.

Her thoughts went back to the recent murder. Maybe she should look into it a little more when she got back to the station. The crime didn't happen in her area but she couldn't shake the feeling of this not being the last. Jasmine's age didn't sit well with her either. The girl was only a few years younger than Sam. She should be living her life to the fullest not tossed like garbage.

"Yo, Walker, when you gonna put some rims on that bad boy? I know that's what I would do." A young man with unkept hair wearing a throwback jersey that was way too big and pants darn near hanging down to his knees admired her car.

"Put some rims on it? Jermaine, I have never known you to have a valid license. You putting some rims on anything would be for it to sit inside the impound." She smiled at the late teen. "How's your grandmother doing?"

He shoved his hands in his pockets. "She good. Working too much as usual."

"Now, she wouldn't have to if you actually had a job."

"I do."

"On these streets all night? This is no way to survive." She opened her door and climbed inside. "Make sure I don't see you any more tonight. Much as I love your family, I will lock you up if you even think about selling drugs while I'm on duty and you know it will break your grandmother's heart."

"Then don't lock me up." He gave her a sly grin.

"Only if you stay off the streets."

She closed the door and fired up the Charger. Her mind needed to be on her beat and not the girl's death on the news.

Chapter 2

Sam finished working out in the police station gym and shoved her bag in the locker. The day before turned out longer than expected on behalf of a domestic dispute: a wife knocked her husband upside the head with a folding chair for something she saw on a social networking site. Then the boys at the barbershop paid a crack head five bucks to run naked down Martin Luther King Jr. Drive. A few club fights were mostly what she'd anticipated.

"Walker, you training for a body building contest or something?" asked a female with a boyish haircut. She leaned on the locker a few down from Sam's.

"Screw you, Maxis." She slammed the metal door shut.

Maxis had been an irritant, no better than an unwanted pebble in a shoe from the day Sam stepped foot in the door. As a woman, Maxis had been used to outdoing all the other females and most of the men. When Sam came along, that changed. Not that Sam made it a point, but it was just who she was. She lived for physical fitness tests and training days to show her skills.

"Oh, so you're working off some stress. Maybe you should try having sex sometime."

"Because you are just getting so much. When was the last time you had a girlfriend?"

"Corporal Walker! Captain wants to see you in his office ASAP," a male shouted into the locker room.

"You are so lucky." Maxis sneered.

"Lucky that I'm not interested in you?" Sam sidestepped her as she crossed over a low wooden bench.

"You? Please. I like mine feminine and you are far from it."

She flipped Maxis the bird and stormed out the locker room. The last report she'd turned in had been gone over with a fine tooth comb. Having to redo almost everyone for the first six months on the force had taught her that lesson so it was no telling what the captain wanted now. She only hoped it wasn't him trying to make her apply for Sergeant again. Sam didn't want a desk job. The streets were her home.

As usual, none of the guys in the station had much to say to her when she passed them in the hallway. It had been this way ever since her incident with Detective Hastings. It wasn't really a physical incident, more of him running off at the mouth after she'd dumped him. He'd come close to a punch to the face courtesy of the right hook she'd held back from swinging.

The captain's office was directly in the center of activity. He often said he preferred it that way so he could keep a good eye on everyone. Standing about six foot three inches and in the neighborhood of 230 pounds, Captain Davis put fear into many of men, but he didn't scare her one bit. She knew the way to his heart: her mother's apple pie on the holidays.

"You wanted to see me, Captain?" Sam poked her head inside his open door. She never felt quite right walking on in.

Someone already occupied a seat in his office. It was a woman and her back faced the door.

"Yes, Corporal Walker, come on in. We were just talking about you." The captain leaned back in a chair that must have been a strain to hold him. Not fat but he was a massive man nonetheless.

"You were?" Sam glanced at the beautiful blonde-haired woman sitting in the chair in front of his desk. She wore a cream-colored suite with a blue shirt underneath and had on natural-toned Red Bottom shoes. Sam only knew they were Red Bottom's from an episode of one of those Real House Wives shows. The show had become a guilty pleasure to relieve the stress of the job. Those shoes were not cheap by any means.

"Indeed we were. Corporal Walker, this is Erica Bellamy, the owner of Pleasures."

"Nice to meet you." Sam gave the woman a half smile.

"Shut the door and have a seat."

She closed the door as instructed.

"As you know, there has been a string of murders amongst the Adult Entertainment Industry."

She nodded.

"Ms. Bellamy here owns one of the biggest clubs, and two of those girls were her employees. We need someone to go in undercover."

"So you want me to check out a few potentials for you?" she asked.

"No, we have already selected our person."

Now she was confused. If they already had someone in mind, then why the heck were they talking to her?

"I have looked through several photos of police officers, but when I saw you walk in the building, I knew you were the perfect choice," Erica said.

"Me? This has to be a joke, right?" Sam wasn't on vice nor was she a detective.

"Not at all," the captain said.

"What about Mills or Hernandez? Even better, Avery works in narcotics so this would be right up her alley."

"None of them have the look I need." Erica's green eyes were on her, inspecting her. She looked Sam up and down from head to toe.

"What look do you need to work the door?"

"You won't be on the door," the captain answered.

Her left eyebrow involuntary rose. "No way, Captain. You want me waiting tables?"

"A little more than that. You will be posing as a dancer."

Fight or flight built up in her core, but she pushed it down and remained seated. She wanted out of that office bad. "Dancing? You mean dancing and wearing those skimpy outfits and stilettos?" Images of stumbling in two-inch heels at prom flashed before her.

Erica beamed. "That's exactly what I need. I need someone to get close to this guy in order to narrow down a suspect."

"Do you mind if I asked why you picked me?" The whole plan didn't sit right with her.

"You're kind of rough around the edges, but with those high cheek bones and that beautiful hair you have pulled up into a bun, I see some potential." The woman eyed Sam as if she were a contestant applying for Top Model. "With my help, you will blend right in."

Sam laughed. "Oh, I seriously doubt the blending part. I'm hardly the girly girl."

"No, you're perfect. You mind me asking what's your nationality?"

"Black," she said flatly.

"What? All this time I thought you were Puerto Rican or something." The captain stared at her with his mouth wide open. "When you say black, you mean like Tiger Woods?"

"No, I mean black as in black as you can get. Both of my parents are black, and both are a few shades darker than me. My grandparents on both sides were also black."

This wasn't the first time someone questioned her ethnicity. She was one of the whitest black women you would ever run into. Biracial people were darker than her, and so is a white girl with a spray tan. Sam could probably have passed for white during times of slavery. On top of it, she had hair down to the middle of her back and all of it belonged to her—no extensions required. Though, no one really got to see it as she normally wore it in a bun.

"It doesn't make a difference to me. My customers would think you are whatever they want you to be and pay top dollar for it. I'd taken you for black and Asian or something."

The captain and this woman had lost their minds. Sam undercover and working at a strip club as a dancer? She would wind up knocking out anyone who dared to touch her. The only way Erica could have pulled this off and so fast was a big payday for the precinct. No way the higher ups would have moved this fast. Not for a club owner and definitely not for some dead strippers. May God rest their souls.

"What about ethics, Captain?" Sam asked.

He didn't flinch. "Ethics? You're going undercover. Undercover means you do what it takes to make the case. It's a gray area. I'm in charge, and believe me, I won't be stepping foot in the club. No offense, Ms. Bellamy."

"None taken," she replied.

"This isn't your average gentleman's club. There is no stripping in the open. From what Ms. Bellamy tells me, the main area looks like a regular club. Stripping isn't illegal, but killing girls is."

"Understood, Captain."

His fingers drummed his desk. "It's settled then. Tomorrow, you report to Pleasures, and I expect a full report within forty-eight hours."

Someone turned a vacuum on her life force and sucked it right out of her. Her happy world had just been shattered. Sam walked out of the captain's office with a look of despair on her face. All eyes were on her as she made her way from the room. The inquisitive stares bore into her flesh. She was sure everyone thought she'd been reprimanded. Oh, how she wished she had.

Chapter 3

The reflection in the chrome on the light casing showed soulless eyes behind a leather mask looking down on a woman. Shrill cries from the latest victim did nothing to stop the torment.

A petite woman laid spread eagle and bound to a metal mortician's table. Though covered in blood and dirt, the brunette, green-eyed woman was beautiful.

"Scream all you want. No one will hear you." A raised hand swooped down, stabbing the victim's left breast.

More high pitched screaming.

The killer continued stabbing and slicing until the contents were able to be freed. One more stab and he withdrew the knife with a silicon implant attached. This breast now matched the other.

The brunette's eyes rolled to the back of her head.

Mr. X grabs a compression pad and duct tape off the tray. With one hand on the pad and the other on the tape, he secures it to her chest to slow the bleeding.

"Oh, no, you don't. I'm not finished with you yet."

Mr. X's hand reached to the side again and selected a syringe off a tray. He jammed it into the victim's heart. With an injection of epinephrine forced into her blood stream, the victim's eyes widened and screaming once again filled the room.

"Are those contacts?" The mask moved in for a better view. "Oh, but they are. Those will have to go as well."

Selecting a smaller scalpel, the hand moved in for the next extraction. In one swift movement, the eyeball along with the optic nerve was removed. The look of terror is frozen in place on the scalpel as the woman lay dead.

"Tsk, tsk. I must've gone in too deep. I better be more careful the next time."

Sam's personal white Charger rolled to a stop in front of Pleasures. From the exterior, she could tell Erica wasn't one for doing anything half assed. The three-story oversized brick building held the name of the club in pink bold letters on it, tilted at a forty-five degree angle with the silhouette of a woman, hands to her lips as if saying "shhh" next to it. A black awning covered the entrance, and a red carpet extended on the walkway.

She took note of the valet parking but parked her car in the semi empty parking lot, which, in a few hours, she assumed would be full. Stepping out of the car, Sam cursed the captain for assigning her to this place. There were others to choose from yet he decided to go with her. She didn't buy the whole she looked the part comments. Something else was up but she just didn't know what.

The captain rushed her off into the case without so much as a peek into the file. His excuse, to keep her focused on the task at hand.

She crossed the parking lot and headed for the door. It flung open when she reached up to knock on it.

"Right on time!" Erica flashed a near perfect smile. "Come on in."

Sam followed her inside the club. From the cameras she observed outside the place, she concluded Erica spotted her pulling in. Even with the lights all the way up, the business resembled a fantasy. The place was in contrast to the hole in the wall she and the other officers frequented. She counted three bars: two on the lower level, one up. Black decorative stone flooring with "Pleasures" sketched in pink lettering sporadically throughout covered the walk way. The bar stools were black and had the club name written on them as well. Pink square couches lined the wall with white leather ottomans positioned in front of a few.

Just like the captain said, there were no stripper poles. Instead, a large dance floor lay stationary in the center of the room positioned about two feet higher than the main level. It had a two-level step wrapping all the way around it. The upper echelon of the club sat open overlooking the lower floor, making for optimal visualization.

They passed a few employees in black and pink uniforms going about their routine of setting up. Even Erica was dressed in a fitted black t-shirt with "Pleasures" written on it and black jeans. Sam felt out of place in her blue V-neck shirt and jeans. As they headed farther into the club, they neared a six foot two inch Italian male, top heavy with muscles. Her breath caught in her throat.

Sam's brain stopped processing the club and flashed back to childhood memories in her best friend's home. A smaller, skinner Vincent Hunter had smiled at her as she and his sister ran past and up to her room.

"That's Vincent, my head of security," Erica said over her shoulder to Sam.

What in the world is he doing here? Last she knew, he was a detective a few years back and then he moved away.

Erica stopped at a door and swiped a key card through the reader. On the other side was a room full of monitors, a state of the art computer, expensive desk, and chaise lounge. All the furnishings were top of the line and included pink studded trimmings.

"Nice." The beauty of the interior moved her mind away from Vincent for the moment.

"So you do speak?" Erica smiled as Sam took in her office.

"Sorry. I tend not to talk when I'm processing my surroundings. It helps me remember everything and everyone a lot better."

"Well, come on in and have a seat." She held out her hand, ushering Sam inside.

Sam almost missed the edge of the chair and hit the floor because she couldn't take her gaze off the monitors. On screen two, images of a scantily clad blonde beauty flashed before her. The entertainer's slow movement captivated Sam. The man sitting on the couch in the room with the woman leaned in closer. She swayed her hips from side to side as she undid her top and let it slide to the floor. More hip rolling and off came her thong.

Hell no. The captain did not expect her to do this. Sam needed to get out of there.

"Excuse me." She pushed out the chair and ran out into the hallway, yanking her phone out her pocket as she went. She pushed three for speed dial.

"This is Captain—"

"Captain, there is no way I'm going through with this. Those girls are naked! I can't do this."

Vincent turned the corner and headed down the hall toward the office. He smiled at her, and she felt like a school girl all over again. The gesture momentarily calmed her panic. Whenever he was home and she visited Kara, she couldn't stop the butterflies in her stomach. Vincent was four years older, and all the girls fawned over him, including her.

Sam almost fainted when Kara and she went to their first homecoming. He was home from college visiting and mentioned how great Sam looked in her dress, even with the Chuck Taylors she wore because she refused to put on heels. The memory made her blush. She dropped her head a moment. When she looked back up, their eyes locked. His gaze said nothing, yet everything. It was the same one she gave back. He'd missed her as she did him.

He gave her a nod and continued on his way.

"Samantha, calm down. I don't expect you to get nude, but I do expect you to at least fake like you would. This is the only way we can get anyone close enough to find out who this nut job is. Didn't you see the news this morning?"

"No, why?"

"There was another body found. This one was mutilated. The breast implants were removed, and the coroner assessment concluded it happened prior to death with no anesthetics."

Sam stood speechless. His baritone voice echoed his last words.

"Sam?"

"I'm here."

"The killer is evolving."

He removed a key card from his pocket and swiped it before disappearing into a room a few doors down. The story Erica came up with about seeing her walk through the door was a sham, it had to be. Vincent knew she was on the force. Him working there couldn't be a coincidence.

"I'll do it," she said to the captain.

"Good. Keep your eyes open."

"Don't I always?"

After ending the call, she walked back into the office.

Erica's eyebrows knitted together. "Are you all right?"

Sam nodded and sat down.

"I know this can be a bit much to take in if you're new to the industry. Rest assured, my girls are not having sex with any of the clients." Erica maintained direct eye contact as she spoke. The wringing she did of her hands was to be expected. It showed her stress. She didn't appear to be lying, but Sam felt she was holding something back. "To be honest, I'm very scared for their safety. The one found this morning wasn't from my club but the strip club down the street. The girl did work here at one point but didn't make it past her probationary period. She drank too much on her shift and couldn't control herself. Why…how could anyone do this?"

Sam sat stone faced. "There are sick people in this world. I'll do my best to blend in and help get this asshole behind bars. My guess is it's someone frequenting the clubs." She'd never been this involved in a murder case. The closest to one was being first on the scene, but she would give it her all.

Erica put her hand to her chin and rocked back as if contemplating something. "If we're going to make you fit in, one of the first things you'll need is a stage name."

"A stage name?" Sam groaned on the inside and hoped she didn't plan on calling her anything like Candy or Cherry.

"No one uses their real name in this industry. How about Mystic?"

Sam frowned. "As in the flavored drink?"

Erica grinned. "No, like the X-Men character. We'll kind of a play off it because hers is Mystique but you get the point. It describes what we're trying to get you to do—blend in—and fits your racial ambiguity. Mystic can be anyone you want her to be."

Sam shrugged. "Sure. I'm fine with it." She could not care less about a name. Her focus was on how in the world she would survive walking in stilettos while checking out suspects.

"Mystic it is then. Can you dance?"

"I haven't since college, but I do have rhythm." She couldn't recall the last time anyone in the cop bar danced. Drinks tended to be the main goal after a rough week.

"Have you ever danced for anyone? Your man? Girlfriend or whomever?"

"No. And I'm not a lesbian."

"I wasn't insinuating you were. Girls do dance for each other, and they're not lesbians." She laughed. "Come on. I'll show you what I mean."

She walked around the desk and headed out the door. Sam followed her through entrance and down the hallway.

"We have ten private rooms back here." Erica led her past the room Vincent entered. Each room had a gold number on them. Erica stopped in front of number five and opened the door. "All rooms are set up the same. Four through seven are a little larger because they're in the center of the hall."

A black love seat sat against the back wall with a hot pink fluffy rug in front of it. A small black leather stool lay along the left side of the room. On the right was a cherry red wooden vanity. The look was finished off with three black and white exotic pictures on the wall. "This is actually very nice."

"What were you expecting?"

"I guess I've been a cop too long. I had images of pay by the hour seedy hotel rooms in my mind."

"As you can see, this is far from it. I like to keep things looking nice to ensure my high-end customers keep on returning. But, as I said before, there's no sex. The gentlemen pay to see you naked, and that's it." She moved behind the vanity. A moment later, a seductive R & B tune Sam heard on the radio before played. "Have a seat on the couch."

Sam made use of a box of baby wipes from the small stand next to the couch and wiped down the leather before sitting down. It looked clean, but she'd seen supposedly clean hotel sheets show all sorts of stuff, to include bodily fluids, once held up under an ultraviolet light. She fanned the area dry before plopping down.

"The name's Ecstasy." Erica appeared from behind the vanity.

And what the hell was Ecstasy doing in here with me? Sam raised an eyebrow.

Erica slow walked toward her. She strategically placed one leg in front of the other as she moved across the room, reminiscent of a lioness on the prowl. Ecstasy stopped in front of Sam. The beat of the music changed, and she threw her hands up in the air and popped her hips to the side. Following the rhythm, she drew one leg up, extended it out, and set it back down. Then she began rolling her hips.

A sense of hypnosis overtook Sam. The swaying of Ecstasy's hips had her locked in a trance. Erica pulled off her shirt and she worked her body. Her flat stomach moved in tune with her hips. She turned her back to Sam and did a body roll as she bent over and tossed her blouse to the floor. Making a small spin, she faced Sam again and moved in closer. Ecstasy place her left leg up on the couch but had her body angled over Sam. She did a few hip thrusts and then brought her body down in Sam's lap.

She rolled her body against Sam. Sam's face flushed, and she squirmed. The heat between Sam's legs rose. She shifted in her seat, uncomfortable with the connection and embarrassed by the slight arousal. The music softened. Ecstasy slid to the floor and the song ended.

Sam's mouth flew open.

"Your turn." Ecstasy's lips curled into coy grin.

Unable to speak as she willed her body to calm down, Sam pointed to herself.

"Yes, show me what you got," Ecstasy said, her tone dead serious. She took a seat and leaned back into the soft leather. "This is how I interview my girls. I need to see what skills you have, and then we can work on what you don't have."

Swallowing hard, Sam rose up off the couch. No way she could do everything Erica had done. As the next song began, images of Jamie Lee Curtiss in the movie *True Lies* flashed in her head. If her nerdish character could do it, then so could Sam.

Sam inhaled and let it out. This was simply an act. *Just feel the music.* She closed her eyes in an effort to take in the instrumental sounds. Her heart pounded against her chest, the beating so loud it almost drowned out the music.

Mustering up the courage, she stuck a hip out to the right then swayed it back to the left.

"Feel me," the sultry voice of the artist called out over the slow tempo.

Sam took it as a cue and slow walked her hands from the top of her body on down, as if exploring herself for the first time. She opened her eyes but didn't make eye contact, forcing herself to continue. Her body stayed in rhythm to the beat.

The song faded out. Three minutes and forty-five seconds dragged out to an eternity. Sam's body was drenched in sweat as she came to a halt and finished up her impromptu routine.

"Not bad." Erica clapped. "Now let me give you a few lessons."

For the next hour, she went over dance moves with Sam. Erica left nothing out in her determination to make Sam fit in with the rest of her girls.

Vincent's glance passed over the men he was giving instructions to the monitors behind him. No longer the gangly adolescent but a full-grown woman rolled her hips from side to side on the screen.

"You want Charles on the door tonight?" the tallest of the three asked. He smirked at the shorter stout guy to his right.

Sam bent over, giving the camera a perfect view of her firm round bottom. No other entertainer ever garnered his attention, but when Sam's butt cheeks spilled out the boy short underwear she wore, Vincent almost lost all motor functions. He coughed, dislodging a response from his throat, and tore his eyes from the monitor. "Yes, Charles, you'll be on door tonight. If you can handle it with no problem, then we'll eventually let you work inside. For now, you have those roaming eyes and I need you to be focused on the patrons, not the girls. Zack and Jon, you guys know the drill. The two of you decide who's working VIP. That's all I have for now."

"What about the stuff on the news?" Jon's thick eyebrows rose.

"What about it?" How the situation was handled didn't concern them.

"Do you think it will affect business?"

"Dancers are being murdered not patrons. As long as the clients have half naked women to look at, nothing will stop them from coming in once the doors are unlocked."

"Geesh, how sick do you think people are?" Zack clutched the cross connected to the long chain he wore around his neck.

"Very. Now go ahead and get set up for tonight." He nodded toward the door.

The three took the hint and excused themselves.

Vincent's mind flashed back to 1996. *He watches from the top of the stairs as detectives talk to his father, his eavesdropping too late to catch the beginning of the conversation.*

The male hands his father a picture. His dad's hand trembles and the photo falls to the floor.

Vincent leans in closer but can't see what's on the photo. At fourteen he knows better than to interrupt adults.

"No." He shakes his head, denying whatever is on the photo.

"We're so sorry." The female reaches out to console him and he pulls away.

Soon the detectives leave and Vincent watches through tear-stained lids as the strong patriarch of the family is reduced to a sobbing lump on the floor.

He rushes down the stairs to check on his father but soon he too would need comforting.

Days later, they attend his mother's funeral. Vincent fights his own emotions while trying to console his sister. Their father drowned his woes in Scotch, refusing to accept the circumstances of the love of his life's untimely death and staying tight lipped with Vincent and his sister regarding the official report.

Chapter 4

Sam wiped the loose strands of hair out of her face as she stepped into the hall. Erica had already made her way back to her office, and Sam needed a break from the practice. *Why couldn't dancing be a simple as firing a weapon?* She strolled down the hall toward the main bar for a much needed glass of water.

"You looked great."

The deep voice stopped Sam in her tracks. A smile spread across her face, and she turned around. Vincent leaned against the frame of the security door. Giddiness from her youth toyed with her adult senses from him being so close to her.

Her smile faded as the reality of his words set in. "I didn't know I had an audience."

"It's what I'm paid to do." He pointed to the camera in the hall. "We're always watching. The boss wouldn't have it any other way."

His revelation didn't make her feel any better. Heat radiated up her neck. Being next to him felt like standing in a sauna. *Get a grip on yourself, girl. You're not a teen.* She made a mental note to give her best friend Kara an earful the next time they spoke. Why in the world had she kept Vincent being back in the city a secret?

"I see." Her voice cracked. Sam's throat went dry, and she was now thirstier than she had been from practicing the dance movies. The questions she had for him would have to wait. She didn't have the time, and this wasn't the place.

"I'll leave you to it then. I'm sure you've been given strict orders." Vincent stepped away from the wall and headed in the opposite direction.

He'd saved her from looking the complete idiot. She glanced at the bar down the hall. Girls lingered around it. Their nationalities spanned the globe, and they all had one thing in common—they were gorgeous in their own right.

It surprised her to see they all looked normal. Due to their profession, she assumed they would be walking around in booty shorts with their boobs hanging out their shirts, like the young girls who walked around the neighborhood on her beat.

Sam felt out of sorts without her badge and gun. She swallowed hard and continued on.

"What do you need?" A tall, athletic-built woman set a box of beer on the counter. "I'm Jenna the head bartender, and this is my area."

"Water..." She hesitated, remembering the name she'd been given. "Mystic."

The woman tossed her a bottle. Sam caught it and nodded a thank you. None of the girls in the area said a word to her as she walked back to the room. It was high school all over again. Ignore the new girl until you find out if she's cool or not.

Sam rolled her eyes and pushed open the door. She'd rather stay in there until it was absolutely necessary to venture out. To her surprise, the room hadn't been left alone while she was away. On the couch laid an outfit and next to it a woman.

"Hey. I'm Ann. I'm here for your makeup and hair." The petite woman tapped the chair in front of her and stood.

Sam had to give it to Erica. All the bases were covered. "I'm Mystic."

It felt like prom all over again as Sam eased in the seat and allowed Ann to do her job. Thankfully she wasn't tender-headed. Ann's heavy hands yanked and curled Sam's hair to perfection before applying the makeup.

Without another word, the woman finished and excused herself. Sam wondered if model's endured the same torture day in and out for photo shoots. The process was overwhelming and all to pretend to work there.

Sam changed into the outfit provided and was ready for her first night on the job. The chrome clock on the small stand read 4:35pm. Her reflection in the metal caught her attention. The person was barely recognizable. Thick curls cascaded past her shoulders. The gold eye shadow and eyeliner made her brown eyes seem a little lighter. A white mini-dress hugged all her curves, and for the moment, she maintained her balance in the four-inch stilettos. Time was ticking, and she needed to be at a meeting in ten minutes. She gave up ogling herself and made her way out the room.

"Looking good, girl." A tall interracial woman smiled at her. Her heritage appeared to be a mix of Japanese and black.

Sam blushed at the beauty walking past her. From the eavesdropping at the bar, she recalled her name as Jade. She had walking in stilettos down to a science. Sam envied the way she strutted. Thankfully, Erica had mercy on Sam and supplied her with wider heels than those attached to Jade's dainty feet. If not, she'd be flat on her rump and not carefully walking down the hallway to the outside of Erica's office.

Most of the nine girls were grouped off talking amongst themselves.

Erica stepped out of her office and wasted no time getting started. "As you all know, Danger is no longer working with us. I found out she'd been screwing customers outside the club. I know you're all young and can do whatever you please, but when you're in my house, it's my rules. You make enough money without sleeping with them so why take the risk? You could get a disease or worse. Don't you watch the news?" She looked around and made eye contact with each of them. "Don't be stupid by getting greedy. Not only will it cost you your job, but it may just cost you your life."

Silence fell over the hallway. From the way Erica carried herself, Sam took it that everyone was used to girls being fired but not the last part of her statement.

"For those who didn't meet her yet, the new girl is Mystic. Skylar," she glanced at a deeply tanned girl, "she'll be your shadow on the floor. Show her the ropes."

"Sure thing, Boss Lady," the girl responded in a slight Spanish accent.

"That's all I have for tonight. Go work the floor."

Work the floor? It's only five.

"You ready, Mystic?" Skylar batted her hazel eyes.

"As I'll ever be." She tried not to sound too sarcastic.

The girls came from behind the black metal door to be greeted with a room full of people. It was happy hour. The other girls split up and began mingling. Sam's heart raced against her chest.

"Let's go to the upstairs bar." Skylar grabbed her hand.

"I really don't feel like drinking."

She looked at Sam and rolled her eyes. "You really are a newbie, huh? We're not drinking. That is, unless someone is buying. We go because that's where the men will be. Upstairs is normally where the big spenders are. *Vamos, chica.*"

"Oh." From that moment on, Sam decided to shut up and learn.

She followed Skylar's lead as she made her way up the stairs. Sam couldn't see it earlier but along with the bar overlooking the club was a nice lounge area. Placed in the center, an elaborate upscale buffet. She spotted caviar and shrimp kabobs. Skylar bypassed the buffet and led her over to a group of gentlemen sitting in leather lounge chairs toward the back of the area.

———

Vincent took his position in front of the black door, the barrier to the backrooms that remained closed during business hours. He placed a tablet on the small stand along with a small device to swipe credit cards and assumed his station as the gatekeeper. This position offered him a perfect view of the front of the house.

The up-tempo music blared through the speakers, enough to keep the patrons happy and not enough to make him want to slit his wrists. Men and woman filled all of the available seating. Just as Vincent expected, a full house. No one cared that a dancer was dead. He doubted the regulars, if any of them, would miss Jasmine. She was simply a pretty face among many. Her clientele will find comfort in the arms of another girl.

Though he regarded her in the same aspect as the other dancers, she'd be missed. It bothered him to go on without given her a moment of silence but doing so would give Mr. X more time for another victim. He'd morn all the girls once the bastard was behind bars.

He took pause at the image on the tablet showing Sam upstairs in the VIP area. Seeing her earlier almost found his tongue running around the ridges of her collar bone. *Dammit! What am I doing? She's my sister's best friend. Stay focused.* The passage of years hadn't squelched the feelings he had for her. Wherever Kara went, Sam was sure to follow, and in his early years as a cop, he made frequent visits to the house to check on them.

His manhood hardened at the image of her breasts poking out through the flimsy material. He made a quick adjustment and got his head out the gutter. They both had a job to do, and his was to protect Sam, not bed her.

A devious smile attached to a flawless—no doubt hidden by makeup—beauty sauntered her way over to him, holding a man's hand, whose eyes were fixated to the voluptuous paid-for rump swaying side to side as she moved.

"How much time?" She flipped her long strawberry blonde locks over her shoulder and turned to the gentleman behind her. "Harold?"

Sweat formed at his brow. Vincent noted the hesitation. He'd hit a dilemma, his wallet versus the supple round ass of the woman in front of him. Feeling no pity for him, Vincent addressed him directly. "How long do you to want to be with her? If you're having second thoughts, it's fine, but Natalie will find time with another gentleman."

His brow furrowed. He ran his wedding ring branded stubby fingers across the massive bald patch on the top of his head. "Three songs…I think that's what we discussed." He dug in his wallet for his credit card and handed it to Vincent.

"Don't worry. The charge shows up on your card as PS Media. Your wife won't have a clue you were here." Vincent handed him back the card and pushed the button, granting them access. "Enjoy and feel free to tip inside the room."

Natalie winked at him as she and her guest disappeared behind the door, and would stay there for the next half hour or so.

"Here's your usual." A waitress handed him a bottle of water from off her tray. "Nice crowd." Her eyes saddened. "Jasmine's mother put her funeral arrangements on Facebook. If you plan on attending, I'll text you the information."

"Thanks, Tina. Of course I'll attend."

A tear welled up in her eye.

He understood her pain. Jasmine was well liked around the club. "She was your best friend. Why are you here? Erica told you to take as much time as you needed."

"Because I can't be home. She's not there. The apartment is so…empty."

He cupped her chin with his hand and lifted up her head. “Whoever did this is not going to get away with it. Look into my eyes and tell me I’m lying.”

She glanced at him. “I believe you.” Tina sniffed.

“If you’re going to be here, you have to pull it together. This is where people come for a good time. There’s no room for tears in this industry. You’re better off hearing it from me than if Erica sees you.” He looked past her at another dancer and her companion waiting to enter the back rooms. “Thanks for the drink, Tina.”

She took the hint and walked off, making her rounds to the patrons.

“Dr. Barnes, it’s nice seeing you again,” Vincent said to the gentleman. “How much time tonight?”

The man slid Vincent his black American Express card. “An hour.” He spoke through perfect veneers.

Dr. Barnes’ blue eyes lit up with excitement as the card met approval.

“I’m going to make sure he enjoys every minute of it.”

“I’m sure you will. Enjoy.” In one motion, Vincent handed him the card and granted them access.

“Hi.” A nervous smile greeted him.

Hands gripped Sam’s tiny waistline, pulling her close. Her neck leaned to the side, opposite of him. Instead of seduction, she oozed discomfort. For his part, the man didn’t notice.

Vincent resisted the urge to peel the man’s fingers off of her. Seeing her like this made him regret bringing her into this mess, but he needed her. He needed someone he would be able to trust, someone to run ideas across without them getting past those very lips, and a woman to cool the soft embers burning in his soul.

The touchy feely man cleared his throat.

"How much time?" Vincent chided himself. He'd lost focus, something he'd never allow to happen.

Not a stranger to the process, the man gladly slapped three crisp one hundred dollar bills on the table. "Thirty minutes should be enough…for now." He gazed at Sam, roaming the length of her curves.

"Enjoy." Vincent barely opened his mouth as he spoke. With regret, he pushed the button and allowed them access.

"Wow, that's fast for a new girl." Jenna's smoke-induced raspy voice pulled his attention away from the closing door. "She's Jasmine's replacement? What's her story?"

"What makes you think I know?"

"Because you're Vincent Hunter and you know all the girls." She smiled, making a small scar under her right eye more noticeable as it scrunched up from her raised cheekbones.

She was pretty enough, but nothing about her stood out like the entertainers. Jenna chose well in choosing bartending over dancing. Besides, by now, she'd be in retirement. The only place a dancer over forty could get work was at the Clermont Lounge, the oldest strip club in the city. By old, he meant age of the entertainment.

"Well, I haven't gotten to know this one yet. If you'll excuse me." He waited for her to head off before speaking into his ear piece. "Zack, I need you to work the back rooms for a moment."

With a half explanation to Zack when he arrived, Vincent left his post and rushed to the security office. He had to see Sam's first show and to know she could handle herself.

Chapter 5

Vincent tossed his keys on the counter and yanked open the small doors beneath it. He was finally home after a long day. It had been months since he'd taken a drink, not that he'd been in rehab but he preferred a clear head. Not tonight.

Whatever possessed him to storm into the security room and watch Sam's first show had been a mistake. At least he'd been smart enough not to watch on the tablet. He'd barely been able to contain his reaction by himself let alone in a room full of people.

The strong liquid burned his throat as he threw the glass back. He slammed it down and poured another shot. *What the hell was I thinking?* He'd made a mistake in requesting her.

He'd gotten to the security room just as Sam came from behind the makeshift changing area. No longer in her dress, her voluptuous chest and ass could barely be contained in the bikini-like lingerie.

Eager hands rubbed together, the man delighted in his choice for the evening. He sat upright on the couch, ready for his show to begin. Sam's musical selection was a stark contrast from the bass driven music playing at the front of the house. The sounds emanating from the speakers in the room were much slower and seductive.

Sam took her time and did a similar routine from earlier, only this time with more confidence. She'd flipped the switch and called on her alter ego. Vincent found himself lost while watching her.

Long legs straddled the man, careful not to rock onto his no doubt hard shaft but close enough for him to enjoy the ride. His hands desperately tried to cop a feel of every inch of her body allowed.

A tongue flicked out. Running along the center of her rib cage, it eased up her neck. Sam arched backward and did a flip onto the floor. With a smooth landing, she seductively pulled the string of the material and unlaced her top. Natural breasts sprang free.

The man's tongue wagged. He became a dog in heat, yearning to get his bitch. She continued with their private party. With each move, she pushed both he and Vincent closer to the edge. Bending over, she gave them a full view of her rump. She trailed a single finger along the thong, running it from the soft puckered mound to the crack of her butt.

As Vincent had seen hundreds of times, the man leaned in, hoping to touch it, taste it, or just get a smell. Sam kept her detachment, allowing for none of the above. Fingers gripped the elastic of the hip bands. She moved them up and down before giving in and sliding the thong off.

Vincent's manhood ripped past his boxers and pushed against the zipper of his pants. Never could he have imagined a more perfect spectacle. His mouth watered.

The timer dinged, and he realized where he was. Vincent snapped out of it. He adjusted his rod up, secured it as best he could behind the belt, and covered it with his shirt. His heart raced as he rushed out of the security office and back to his post.

For the rest of the night, he avoided all eye contact. One wrong move and his friend below would spring up and knock over the table he manned.

The memory of Sam's show faded a bit. Vincent slammed the empty glass on the table and wiped his mouth. *You are a fool.* The thought alone made his rod stiffen again. Alcohol couldn't help him. He needed a cold shower.

Beep, beep. The notification alert on his phone signaled a text message.

Sam: I'm wide awake. Where are you?

Vincent: Home.

Sam: Address please.

Vincent: 259 14th Street.

Sam: On my way. Close by.

Shit! His fingers had a mind of their own. He should have told her no. In less than ten minutes, a fresh-faced, sweat-outfit clad Sam stood outside his open door.

"Man, this is a nice condo." She marveled at his place.

Having company didn't rank high on his priority list. Seeing her reaction made him remember the interior designer he paid to decorate the place. He'd relented into her idea of adding a hint of bright color to his choice of white, black, and gray, so azure accents found their way in the mix.

Sam remained quiet. Her fingers walked along the ridges of his white Italian leather couches, and she smiled at the Asian artwork. She stopped in front of his fireplace where swords were on display. "I'd almost forgotten," she said, her voice barely above a whisper. "You don't really need to work. The trust from your mother when you turned twenty-five." Her eyes locked on his as she spun around. "I'm sorry."

He swallowed hard at the memory. "It's okay."

Sam never had the pleasure of meeting his mother. Vincent and his family moved into another house in another side of the city by the time she'd come along. The new middle school brought her and Kara together. Two new girls at a school, bound by fate.

"What's up?" He shoved his hands in his pockets.

"I didn't get to see you when the club ended." Her eyes searched the floor. "I need to know why you chose me for this. There's no way Erica just happened to come up with my name. Why me? Why for this?"

"Have a seat." He motioned for her to follow into the kitchen. Vincent offered the same chair he'd left out while drinking to her. "This person isn't going to stop until they're caught." He remained standing across from her. The closeness played with his senses. A hint of fresh vanilla wafted up to his nostrils. She'd showered.

She sighed. Her glare caught him. Fire and determination blazed between them. "I know, but there are several other people who could have handled this. I'm a beat cop."

The look, that's why he'd chosen her. When Sam wanted an answer, she'd go to no end to get it. She'd always been that way, no matter the obstacle. "I don't trust anyone else."

"I know it's girls from the club, but why is it so personal to you?"

Vincent gazed at the ceiling for answers. He'd never admitted out loud, and even now, Sam was like family but she'd only get a partial answer. He wasn't ready to let anyone know how personal this was. "I don't think they got the right person the first time around, or there was more than one killer."

"You think it was a team?" Her forehead wrinkled in confusion. "You're speaking about Reynoldstown, right?"

He nodded. "When the murders started again, Mr. X repeated his message from 2008 at the crime scene. The X with a smiley face next to it on the bottom of the stiletto."

Her lids narrowed in thought. "You really think it's someone who frequents the club?"

"Who knows? It's a start and better than doing nothing." He admired how relaxed she looked. Dressed down was more of her comfort zone. "How'd you enjoy your first day?"

"Okay for the most part." An eyebrow rose. "But, no disrespect there are some creepy ass crackers out there."

Laughter erupted out the pit of his stomach. "None taken. Yes, there are a lot of creeps and a bunch of freaks that cross the threshold."

"I'll never understand any man that wants to lick the sweet spot of a random female."

Vincent warmed under the collar.

"I must have seen at least ten guys tonight," she continued. "They lose their minds in the back rooms. How many girls have broken the rules?"

He cleared his throat. "A few here and there. Erica fires them on the spot. Most don't want to cross her. It won't stop the men from begging for it though. That's what the girls are there for. Let the men think they can have something they never will."

"What made you work there of all places?"

He thought long and hard. "I found myself not being able to go back to the department, and the club allowed me to maintain a low profile while I sorted some things out."

"I see." She tapped the display on her phone and the light came on. "It's getting late. I have my answer so now I'll let you get some rest."

"I'll walk you out." *Thank God.* Anymore talk about the club and he'd be the one begging for a taste. He walked to the door and turned to say his goodbye before allowing in the night air. Her mouth mere inches from his, everything went in slow motion. His breathing slowed as she sucked in the bottom lip. For moments, they stayed that way.

"I guess I'll see you tomorrow." She wrapped her arms around him, giving him her usual goodbye hug from long ago.

"Yeah, tomorrow." He opened the door and saw her out. She stepped through, and he closed it behind. "About that shower…" he muttered to himself.

Chapter 6

A slight grin spread across Sam's face as images of Vincent invaded her mind once again that afternoon. Was it her school girl crush or had he, too, felt something last night? He'd been so close. Any movement and their lips would have locked.

She whipped her car into the station's parking lot, and all giddiness slipped away. Ex-cop or not, he'd still worn the badge and the last relationship she had with one didn't fair to well. The fallout with Hasting still had her doubting if she'd ever submit her application for detective.

White and black cars were scarce, making for easy parking since most of the station was out doing patrols. Her smile faded as she walked inside and headed to the captain's office. Going undercover had nothing to do with hooking up with Vincent but catching a killer, and she needed to focus in order to give a proper update.

On both sides of the glass, heads popped up from desks like gophers. Sam slanted her eyes at them. *What gives? Why are they gawking?* She only been out the office two days, and they behaved as if she were a new recruit.

She stuck her head inside the captain's door. "You have a moment? I'm here for my forty-eight hour update."

He paused for a second, giving her a once over before responding, "Of course."

She proceeded inside. "What's that look for?"

"Your hair." His brows raised in thought. "I've never seen it down."

She absentmindedly ran her fingers along the bottom of her strands, forgetting she hadn't bothered with the pony tail after such pain staking work to get it to look nice. "I have to look the part."

"I'll admit. Ms. Bellamy knows her girls. "

"Excuse me?"

"Take the compliment." He walked around his desk, his frame towering over her before leaning against the front edge of the wooden structure. "Are you fitting in okay?"

"As to be expected. I have a question though. What about the money?"

"Take it as if you were moonlighting. I dare not ask how much you made, but I'm sure you earned every dime."

Recalling her skimpy-required attire and her newly acquired seductive dance moves, she blushed.

"Any leads?"

The land mind she felt she stepped on had been defused. She didn't want the captain or anyone else in on her embarrassment, or knowing how comfortable she'd gotten with her character by the end of the night. With Skylar's urging and cheerleading, she'd become a client's favorite. She had to in order to get one-on-one time with them to see who could possibly be a suspect.

A knock at the door interrupted them. “Captain?” A man with jet black hair, a chiseled jaw line, and perfect smile stuck his head in.

Sam cast him a glare.

“Hastings. Come on in,” the captain said, his voice a bit excited for Sam’s liking.

He nodded and entered, taking a standing position across the room. Just out of punching in the gut reach for Sam.

“Sam, as you know, Detective Hasting’s been assigned this case from the beginning. He’ll need updates on all the information you have.”

She directed her attention back to the captain, calming the urge to pick a fight with her ex just out of spite. “I was just about to tell you that I’m only now getting the trust of the girls. There’s one who seems to really like me. What I can’t get from the men, I’m sure I can work out of her.”

“Captain,” Hastings butted in. “I don’t really see how Walker being undercover is affective. She’s out of her league and has no training.”

Going for the jugular, I see. Jerk.

“It’s not for you to see, but for the men to believe. I’ve already gotten a report from the owner. Walker is a natural.”

Heat formed around the base of her neck. Sure it probably should be taken as a compliment, but being a natural at getting naked was a bit much.

For the first time since he entered the office, her ex took a good look at her. “You actually can be taken for a female with your hair down.”

Her fingers balled into fists.

"That's enough." The captain crossed his arms. "Hastings, this is technically your case, but unless you can dress up in a thong, then Sam's staying undercover. You need her for information." He directed the next at Sam. "If that's all you have, then go on and head out. No need for you to be here longer than you need to be."

She nodded and made a hasty exit before she could no longer contain herself. Any more time in the room and there'd be an argument.

Vincent meticulously went about preparing for his day. He pressed his finger down on a keypad, and his Philips Saeco kicked into action. Within moments, the aroma of the highest quality of Italian espresso with a rich layer of crema permeated the air.

He left the kitchen to enter a large laundry room and prepped an ironing board. The iron heated up, and steam flew out an expensive iron while Vincent rested his black slacks on the surface.

A timer sounded in the background, and 90's hip hop music floated out of speakers mounted around the entire condo. The pants were ironed to perfection followed by his security shirt. When finished, he took his time laying them on two padded hangers before walking back into the kitchen.

He grabbed his cup and sat in front of his touch screen computer. Fingers flew across the keyboard, and the Atlanta Police Department website pulled up. He entered a password. ACCESS DENIED in bold letters flashed on the screen.

"Suri."

The music stopped playing. "Yes, Hunter?" a computer voice from his phone answers.

"Call the White Rabbit."

"Dialing."

A woman answered on the first ring. "Hunter, whatever you heard, it wasn't me." The female voice cracked with nervousness.

"Calm down. I'm calling in a favor." He laughed. "How good are you at getting into government systems without leaving a trace?"

"The best. I've been doing this since I was seven—"

"I don't need the details. I just need you to hack the department's system and pull a file." As her arresting officer, he knew the White Rabbit, real name Cindy Lee, all too well. At fourteen, she'd hacked into the account of a prominent business man. Her using the school computer was the only way she'd gotten caught. Vincent arrested her and asked the judge for a lesser sentence. Cindy's parents had died and she was left to care for her ailing grandmother, who really needed to be in a nursing home. But, if that were to happen, it would leave Cindy in foster care. At her age, Vincent couldn't bear seeing the young girl put into the system with the possibility of being molested, or worse.

His qualms on her doing the hack were overshadowed by his desire to catch Mr. X. No way he was leaving this up to the department. They had their chance.

"Which file you need?" Enthusiasm spilled through the line. "APD, right?"

Vincent heard fingers at work on a keyboard. "Mr. X."

There was a pause. Then she said, "Whoa. You worked on the case of a serial killer? That's heavy stuff."

"I just need the file."

"Sent."

"How'd you get my… Never mind, I forgot who I'm talking to." He clicked on his email. The file from 2008 and everything current were attached. She'd linked the two together. "Thanks."

"I thought you were no longer a cop. What's this? Light reading?"

"Hardly. I'm just checking into things." He scanned through the images.

"If you ever need me, you know how to reach me."

"Thanks. I have to go." He didn't want to feed into her habit any more than necessary.

The call ended.

The image of a cuffed titanium bracelet attached to the dainty hand of a woman flashed on the screen. His mind went back to his mother and father's anniversary in 1995.

Vincent and his sister sat in an elegant restaurant as their mother opened a small box and pulled the gift out. Her eyes watered as his father slid it onto her wrist.

Ten years later…

Vincent stormed into his childhood kitchen. "Is this what you've been hiding from me all these years?" He thrust a file at his father. "My mother was a call girl? Why'd you stay with someone who'd betrayed us?"

"Son, you don't understand." His father dropped his head.

"No, I don't. You practically worship the ground she walked on and would have me do the same." He took long strides as he paced the kitchen.

"Stop. I won't listen to you bad mouth her."

"You don't have to. It's all in black and white." Vincent stormed out, slamming the door behind him.

He clicked off the file and pressed print. The printer fired up and made noise as its making copies of the case for him to present to Sam. Sam oh Sam. When his thoughts weren't on the case they were on her. He'd have to stick to strictly business if they were going to work together.

Chapter 7

Vincent followed Erica's beckoning into her office. He waited until she was comfortable in her chair, her semi-throne, before questioning her. "How's she working out?"

The green flakes in her eyes lit up. "If she wasn't a cop, I'd ask her to stay. She's a fast learner, and the men love her. Definitely an excellent money maker."

"That good, huh?" Vincent hadn't expected gushing from his boss. Appraisal maybe but Erica was practically salivating at the mouth.

"Should I leave the hiring up to you?"

He gave her a long hard look. Seeking out girls for this line of work was out of his league. Sam was different. They needed her. "You pay me enough for what I do."

"True." She glanced down at a sticky note. "Some NFL players will be in tonight. Brief your guys and I'll let the girls know who gets to work VIP tonight."

Back to a comfortable subject. "I'll get on it." He gave her a nod and headed back to his office to prepare for the evening. Thankfully, he'd hired extra help and all of them were on duty for the night. Players meant bringing them in discreetly through the private entrance and up the backstairs. What the players did once they got them to VIP was on them. Most kept themselves hidden from the rest of the club, but once in a while, you got the ones who need everyone to know they're in the place. Often those were the rookies.

The image of Sam pulling into the back parking lot on the security monitor brought Vincent out his office. He rested his frame against a side wall to wait for her by the rear entrance. This time of the day was the best for them to talk. No prying eyes around.

Through the one-way mirrored glass, he had a clear view of her walking up. The wind whipped at her hair, blowing it away from her face. Calvin Klein's name crisscrossed around her curves as the fitted t-shirt hugged her body. Her long legs extended out, covering the width of the lot with ease.

"Hey." Vincent opened the door before she had a chance to ring the bell.

"Hi." She blessed him with her amazing smile and cocked her head to the side in confusion as to why he waited by the door. "What's up?"

"I have something you need to see. I thought about bringing it here, but I'm not willing to run the risk of you leaving it in the locker room. These girls have ways of getting into each other's lockers. You can pick it up after hours." *And I'll make sure I don't watch any of your shows so I won't come off as a pervy perve.*

"All right, cool."

He took note of her black bag with Starship Enterprises written on the side. "What's that?"

She blushed, and her newly French manicured nails gripped the prized possession. "Something to wear. I noticed the other girls took multiple changes. The outfit Erica gave me is nice, but I need to fit in, right? So style change it is."

"Erica's right. You are a fast learner."

The buzzer sounded behind them. Another model stood waiting at the door.

"I'll leave you to it." Sam smiled again and walked off.

———

Sam patiently waited for the makeup artist to finish her magic. Tonight, she didn't mind it as much. Her cherry had been popped. She'd survived her first night and didn't kill herself in the heels, especially after Skylar gave her the hint of removing them once in the room.

When finished, the woman smiled. Sam handed her a tip, and she went on her way to the next girl in the changing room. The day before had been a luxury of being allowed to get herself together in a private room. Now, she was simply another model and needed to dress with the other girls. It's why she made it a point to get there early. By the time everyone else spilled in, she and the other two early birds were already dressed and ready.

The other girls moved about topless or completely nude, shaven glory on full display as they talked amongst themselves and got ready. Fake and natural breast littered the room. With the help of pushup padding, her B cups fit right in. The men didn't care about the padding once the top was removed, being bare sent them to a whole other dimension.

"So, newbie, how you like it so far?" a brunette asked. Her back faced Sam but her not-so-friendly ice blue gaze on tanned skin could be seen in the mirror she faced.

"Sapphire, is it?" Her antics didn't faze Sam in the least bit.

"Yup. That's me." She attached long dangly earrings to her ears. "Learn your place and stay away from my customers."

"Why? You scared I might stick around? Or they might like me better?" Sam slid off the highchair and walked out, but not before registering the shocked looked on Sapphire's face and hearing the giggles from some of the other girls.

"Hey." Another dancer caught up with her. Underneath the long weave resided a caramel-complexion beauty. "Sapphire's just jealous. She thinks you're white. I know you're not. You just have that Mariah Carey thing going on. She's intimidated by you. I'm Chanel."

"Mystic." Sam gave a silent prayer the girl didn't extend her hand for a shake. Chanel had just shaved her crotch in front of the entire room. There was little doubt she washed her hands after. The thought of someone's vajayjay on her hand grossed Sam out.

"You've made an enemy for life, but that's what she gets." The girl laughed. A dimple formed in her left cheek.

"It wouldn't be the first time." Sapphire may as well have been Maxis. Both exulted the same crazy behavior. Like Maxis, she freaked out when the new girl arrived and tried to flex her muscles. One thing Sam's mother didn't raise was a timid child. In fact, she instilled the no one is better than you, they only think they are, and it's up to you to prove them wrong. Maxis found out the hard way during their self-defense training. Sam slammed her to the ground with ease. Being butch didn't make you a stronger woman. It just made you butch. If Sapphire dare tried anything else, then she, too, would get slammed.

She stopped walking at the main bar and pulled up a seat.

"You need something or are you just resting your feet?" Jenna the bartender glanced up from stocking glasses on a shelf.

"Water please."

"I'll take a Coke." Chanel slid in the seat next to Sam.

Jenna poured the water first then the Coke out of the same pump. Sam appreciated the water being filled first, less chance of mixing in the weird carbonation taste. When finished, she set the glasses on the bar.

"So what's your story?" Jenna asked. Her blue eyes peered into Sam. Those eyes defied her age. There was a sense of sadness or hurt behind them. She'd definitely lived a hard life.

Sure, bartenders were probably used to getting all the latest gossip, but she'd had a better chance of getting a mouse from a snake than Sam spilling her guts. "What makes you think I have one?"

"We all do." Jenna flipped her stringy brown hair over her shoulder. Her makeup was betrayed by the age lines forming at the corner of her mouth.

"Then what's yours?" The unexpected reversal. Sam played this game all too well.

"Where do I begin?" She popped an elbow up on the counter. "I got married to a shitty guy at a young age. He was a loser and couldn't stay out of jail. I needed a job and probably wouldn't make the best waitress so bartending it is. I've been doing it almost twenty years now. Your turn."

"Actually..." Sam eased out the chair, mindful of the additions to the bottom of her feet. "It's time to get to our meeting for the night. Maybe later."

Chanel followed suit and walked to the back of the management area with Sam. Dancers spilled out into the hallway from the dressing room just as Erica walked out of her office for their meeting. She'd changed out of the t-shirt and jeans Sam had seen her in earlier. The high end black club dress and expensive shoes radiated that she was in charge.

She walked to the center of the group and got started. "Okay, ladies, tonight we have celebrity V.I.P.'s coming in."

Eyes lit up with excitement, and a few squeals escaped painted lips.

"I need you all on your best behavior." She made direct contact with a few models, Sapphire being one of them. "Skylar, Mystic, Jade, Chanel, and Barbie, you all will be able to access the celebrity area. The rest of you, don't go near it unless you are specifically requested. If you are, then you need to let me or Vincent know before you saunter your ass up there."

Girls huffed and moaned.

"Why does the newbie get the special treatment?" Sapphire spoke up between pouty lips and crossed arms.

Erica snapped her head in her direction. "Because I'm the boss and what I say goes." To everyone else, she said, "That's all I have, ladies. Have a great money-making evening." She turned on her heels and headed back to her office.

Sapphire brushed past Sam. "The newness will wear off soon enough."

"You should know," Sam spat back, but Sapphire had already put distance in between them as she made her way to the closed doors that kept the area secure from the front of the house.

Sam moved forward but not as eager as the rest of the girls. She didn't care about the clients. There was a killer on the loose and so far she'd only managed to learn new moves, piss off a few dancers, and add money to her bank account.

Once again, the establishment filled up with clients from all walks of life, though the not so well off men lingered near the main bar and kept their distance from the girls. Sam was sure Erica laid down the law in the early days of the club opening.

"You look amazing."

Sam blushed at the deep voice behind her. She turned to face Vincent. "Thanks." A slight breeze grazed across her bottom, cutting right through the sheer material with a whoosh from Vincent closing the door behind him.

"Purple is your color." He went about his routine of setting up his check point area as the gatekeeper.

She had doubts about the ensemble when she selected it off the rack, but it matched the white one provided by Erica so why not? "I better get to work."

He nodded.

Swooning over him wouldn't solve anything as far as the case was concerned. Tonight, she would lay back more and watch the room. A man at the main bar arguing with Jenna caught her attention. The issue was resolved easily when Zack, one of the security guys, tapped him on the shoulder.

Worn dress shoes on the gentleman's feet stood out. He wouldn't get the attention of any of the girls. A thought occurred to Sam. What if the killer was upset because the girls didn't pay him any mind? Would that be enough to murder someone? Years of being overlooked from childhood to now building up until he snaps. She'd keep an eye on him.

She climbed the stairs, making her way up to the V.I.P.. From her perch, she still could keep a watch on him.

"What's wrong, baby? We're not enough for you up here?" A large male leaned up against the railing. His massive frame made it impossible for her not to provide him with her undivided attention.

A fake smile creased her lips. She paused for a moment so a sarcastic comment wouldn't slip out. "I'm sorry. You're more than enough, darling. I just had a few things on my mind."

"Well, you're in luck. I'm here to make all your dreams come true. How does an hour sound?" He popped open a case full of cash and pulled out a stack before handing the case to the supersized man a few feet away from him. The guy snapped the case closed and dropped it to his side.

Like torture. This huge guy needed an even bigger guy as a bodyguard? Sam stifled her laugh. "It sounds great."

His bear paw swallowed her hand as she placed it in his and led him down to the private rooms. Vincent didn't say a word when the guy slammed the stack off money on his work station. He simply pushed the button and waved them on.

By the time Sam finished with the defensive back, she felt like Shaq going into the fourth quarter. Her body was drenched in sweat. How much twerking and booty clapping did one man need? Apparently a lot because he kept asking for more and tipped more than the total she'd made the previous night, which wasn't anything to scoff about.

She glanced at the bar, and her suspect was gone. So much for following up her theory. She'd have to ask around, maybe even play nice with Jenna to get more information on him. Sam was sure she could make up some story to appease the nosey woman.

"Hey, darling. I'll see you in a moment. A girl needs to freshen up." She put on her sexiest voice, ready to free herself from her client now that she had him back in the main area.

"You know where to find me." He winked.

"Hold on. I'll join you." Skylar speed walked over to her. "I'm drained."

"Ditto."

They remained silent until back in the locker room. Sam freshened up with a towelette and changed into a two piece black and gold mini skirt ensemble.

"Great choice. *Muy bonita!*" Skylar slipped on a red extremely high slit dress with a plunging neckline. She put Angelina Jolie to shame with her toned exposed legs. "There's a private party tonight. You've been requested."

"By whom? Erica?" Being in the club was one thing. She wasn't about to get suckered into a prostitution ring. What did the lady think? Sam wouldn't come back and bust her ass later?

Skylar look flustered. Her eyes darted around, ensuring no one else entered the locker room. "No. She doesn't know. Some pretty high up people run this show, though. Lots of money involved. It will be more than enough to buy you some cha cha's if you wanted." She tapped Sam's padded breasts.

"I don't know. I'm new…"

"Don't worry. The problem girls aren't a part of it. I like you and think you'll be perfect."

Sam wondered what exactly made her perfect but didn't want to push. Too many questions and she'd sound like a cop. "Not tonight because I've already made plans. But I'll think about it for the next time." She'd check into it but only after running it by Vincent first.

"Okay. We better get back on duty. Just so you know, that stack you got was about three grand. It's all yours. The house already got their cut."

"And to think I hadn't done this sooner." Sam smiled at the naivetés of the girl. Money couldn't fix that low self-esteem she had. If they just cleared three grand, then why on earth would you go have sex with them? Maybe it was best she didn't understand the mentality.

Sam fell behind to make a pit stop with Vincent. "Did you see where the guy went that sat at the end of the bar?"

"Yeah, back to work. He does maintenance work at the Hilton. This is where he spends his lunch breaks."

"Oh, but I saw him getting mouthy with Jenna, and Zack had to step in." She leaned in so he could hear her without shouting over the music.

"You saw wrong. Zack's his baby brother, and Jenna just gives him a hard time. That's her."

"Back to the drawing board then. I better get back upstairs."

"Hey." Vincent grabbed her hand. "You're doing fine. Just don't focus on the obvious. Killers won't make themselves known. It's the quiet ones we need to keep our eyes on."

She freed her hand from the electrical charge he sent down her spine. "Okay." Sam whisked herself away from him and back to performing her duties. But between dancing and checking for possible suspects, she couldn't stop herself from taking peeks at him. Each time she brought a man back to the room, she pretended he was Vincent.

Chapter 8

Mr. X sat in the car. Waiting wasn't hard. It was the calm before the storm. Every now and then, laughter spilled into the streets as the men filtered out of the house with some whore attached to their arms. The clacking of heels against the sidewalk would be squelched behind the closing of a car door.

He continued watching the house, taking in every detail. The chipped cement at the base of the stairs, the fresh awnings against the windows, and the gold numbers sparkling bright—signaling that yes, this was the right place. The location was only a few streets from the heart of downtown, but far enough before it dare turned into a rough neighborhood. Discreet and quiet. People in this area stayed to themselves and wouldn't question expensive luxury vehicles coming and going.

Moments passed, and the door opened again. Not the person he wanted. When the right one came out, the killer would know, but patience need be exercised. Like clockwork, there he was. Dr. Barnes's brown hair caught in the wind, exposing the slight balding patch at the base of his head. On his arm the strawberry blonde.

His eyes rolled at the stupidity of the man. Jasmine had been his warning, and yet all he did was go back and provide another victim. When they reached the vehicle, Mr. X pulled off. No need to follow. Dr. Barnes hardly made it difficult for who Mr. X's choice of the evening would be. As a married man, he wouldn't be taking her home, and a hotel would be too easy to track. They'd go to her place.

———

Standing in the darkness of the room, dressed all in black and masked, Mr. X waited for the sound of the click. In they stepped. From behind the door came movement, so subtle they didn't notice in their drunken state. Gloved hands holding chemically laced cloth covered both mouths, incapacitating the couple. Mr. X dragged the woman outside while leaving Dr. Barnes in a heap on the floor.

Who would he tell? He'd be admitting to his indiscretion. No, Dr. Barnes would wake and wipe down any trace of him being there. Like the bastard he is, he'd go home, kiss his wife, and wake up the next day without a care in the world.

———

Vincent patiently waited for Sam to arrive. He wanted to give her the packet but also get into her head after spending hours with some of the NFL Players. The ones who came in felt they could have anything they wanted as long as they had cash. The video mentality of making it rain ran rampant amongst those with money and girls who yearned to make it theirs.

Cheese and cracker sat as the centerpiece of his island just in case Sam wanted a light snack after a long night. He checked the time—ten minutes since he'd last checked. If she hadn't insisted on a shower, then he wouldn't be pacing around like a desperate puppy waiting for their human to arrive.

His buzzer sounded. *Finally.*

He took a deep breath and cloaked himself in a cool and calm demeanor, his normal self unless around Sam, and opened the door. A radiant beauty with a shower fresh scent of mangos stood on the other side.

Vincent welcomed her in and stepped to the side for her to pass.

"What? No hug? We're not at the club." Her smile beamed in the dim lighting of the foyer.

"Sorry." He reached over and gave her a half hug, ensuring their bodies didn't fully connect. His member rising up now would only serve to embarrass him. "My mind's on this case."

"Speaking of…where's the file?" Sam brushed past him and walked farther into his home as if she'd been there a million times instead of only once before. She stopped when she reached the couch and slumped down into the soft cushions. "My feet are exhausted. Even out of the heels, they still ache."

"I'll take your word for it." He grabbed the folder off his desk and brought it over to her.

"You mean you have no desire to walk around in shoes not suited for any purpose other than to please a man?" A hand flew to her chest, feigning shock. "Say it isn't so."

He took in how her face lit up. "You're still the little comedian, I see."

"Simply breaking the ice before I jump into this." She cracked open the file. Before her eyes completely registered the grotesqueness of the photos, her facial expression changed. The beautiful smile faded at the corners and fell slack.

Vincent watched intently as she maintained her composure as best she could and continued flipping through the contents of the file. The pictures were easy compared to actually being on the scene. He'd seen death dozens of times and would never get used to it, simply hardened. You push the idea of it once being a person to the deep dark corners of your soul if you wanted to function and be able to solve the case. At least, that's what he'd learned from his mentor and former partner Hank.

He provided no comfort as her eyes welled up until a single tear spilled down the side. This was part of the job. Get it out now so we can get to the next. He needed her to see the horror. The fear and terror needed to register in order to get her in to the right mindset. This was real, in your face, and not a news channel that could be turned. Walking in on a suspect who'd overdosed was nothing compared to this. You don't mourn for the scumbags. Yes, the earlier ones had chosen an illicit profession, but the new ones were girls who she could have seen earlier today…

"Is this Jasmine?" she choked out. Now she was glad the captain had kept the file from her. The girl could have been Sam's younger sister. They had the same facial structure and long black hair.

He nodded at the head shot.

"She looks so innocent. Peaceful almost."

…who worked a job to simply get by in life.

Sam turned the picture over and moved to the next. The pictures fell to the floor as her hands went to her mouth. "Oh my God!"

Vincent intentionally put the new murders in the back. The head shot first then the full body. She had to see the evolution. He'd eased her in and walked her through the sordid eye of Mr. X. There was no need for him to view the photo. Jasmine's disfigured body had been forever imbedded in his mind.

"I knew there'd been torture but this…" Her head shook in disbelief. "Why mutilate her?"

Vincent had thought long and hard about Jasmine's body being stuffed with rotted food to the point of her skin stretching almost being its capacity and then being sewed back up at her belly button. "You need to see the next picture."

Shaky hands reached down and picked up a single photo that flew far to the right because it was the last one left. Her throat muscles flexed as she swallowed hard and took a deep breath. She flipped it open—her eyes frozen in horror.

"That was Amber. She disappeared before Jasmine. She used to work at Pleasure's over a year ago. It doesn't make sense to murder a past employee if the motive is Pleasure's. What I do know is Amber wore contacts, received Botox injections in her lips, had breast and butt implants. All of which have been removed." He pushed off the couch and walked into the kitchen. Sam needed a drink. Hell, he needed a drink. Her going through the files and him watching her as she did sent them both on an emotional roller coaster. He reached into the cabinet and pulled out the black bag with Crown Royal written in gold letters across the front. Vincent removed the crown-shaped thick bottle from it. After filling up two shot glasses, he carried them back over to the couch.

Sam gladly accepted the liquor. She downed it without hesitation. “What is it?” A cough escaped her lips.

“Crown Royal Black.”

She gave him a questioning glance. “I don’t take you for a Crown Royal guy.”

“A habit I picked up from my old partner.” He took his turn at his glass. “Yes, it’s strong.” Hank was a great detective, a father figure, and a good friend. The older black gentleman took him in and showed him the ropes.

“You were about to tell me your take on this.” The horror slipped from Sam’s eyes, replaced by determination.

“Mr. X is removing all of their paid for enhancements. In essence, he’s leaving them as imperfect as they thought they were. This is new.” He leaned back into the couch in thought. “Something has changed.”

“What about the guy they locked up?” Even the mayor proclaimed the Reynoldstown killer gone.

“I never thought it was the guy in the first place. You don’t go from sloppy robberies and bungled aggregated assault to calculated killing. Let’s face it. The guy wasn’t the brightest.” His mind drifts back to 2008.

A rusted iron door slid closed behind Vincent and bolted shut. Now he, too, was locked inside of the Georgia State Prison. He took a seat in the orange plastic chair located in front of the metal table.

Another door opened on the back end of the room. Two guards escorted Mitchell Harold in. Confined by chains and cuffs shackled to his hands and feet, he shuffled inside. The guards maneuvered him to the seat on the other side and locked him to a metal handle protruding out the inmate side of the table.

"Detective," he sneered through rooting teeth, "to what do I owe the displeasure?"

"Who's your partner?" Vincent kept his stoic demeanor as he leaned forward and got eye level with the man who barely stood five feet five inches tall. His rail thin body couldn't have weighed more than one hundred-fifty pounds soaking wet.

"I didn't do it so why would there be a partner?"

"That's the thing in this place. Everyone's innocent."

Mitchell sat as upright as the cuffs would allow. Dirty fingernails twisted along with his wrists to alleviate the metal cutting into his flesh. His eyes, so dark they were almost black, narrowed. "I can't help you with that. I do know one thing, though, Detective Hunter..." His words slowed, echoing around the room. "Your mother was the best piece of ass I ever had." His tongue snaked out, licking across his dry cracked lips.

Vincent's fist pounded against the table as he stood.

"You never know. I could be your daddy, boy." He laughed.

Vincent lunged in his face, stopping short of punching the life out of him. "For that, I will happily be here when the needle is injected into your arm and the breath wasted on you is no more." He turned his head to the door. "Guards!"

They rushed in.

"You okay?"

Sam's voice pulled him out of his thoughts.

"Yes. I'm just thinking. There has to be a pattern outside of the girls working at Pleasures." He stared at the photos long and hard searching for clues, something, anything to stand out. He felt Sam's eyes on him.

"There's something you should know." Her voice was low.

His attention went from the blood-splattered photos to her. "What?"

"I've been approached about a 'private party.' Apparently, some of the girls make big money at these after hours. There's one tonight."

"Why didn't you tell me?"

"I'm telling you now. I had no intention of going. Who knows what's going on there? Dancing is one thing. I'm not sleeping with some random man for money."

"No one expects you to." *And I'd beat them to a pulp for trying.*

She raised an eyebrow. "I'm not going." Her mouth opened wide, letting out a yawn.

"You're tired. Go home and get some rest. We can pick this back up tomorrow."

Sam nodded while stifling another yawn. Vincent walked her to the door and this time allowed himself to give her a real hug. She needed the contact after reviewing the file, and so did he.

Chapter 9

The phone rang. Sam bolted upright, interrupted from her slumber. In a haze, her hands reached for the cell phone resting on her nightstand.

Groggily, she answered, "Hello."

"Thanks for calling me back," her sister's voice quipped.

"Tracey?" Her eyes focused on the time, and she slumped back in the bed. Ten was just too early after going to bed after four.

"I know you're not still sleeping. What's going on with you?"

"Work."

"What else is new? Are you coming to the party or not?"

"Jesus. I'm not even functioning yet, and you're on my back." Tracey didn't deserve the attitude, but she was tired. All morning long, her dreams were haunted by images of her walking up on crime scenes and finding dead bodies. "I have this case…"

"See there you go. It's always about you and work. You're so busy worrying about other people's lives but not your own family!"

"What are you talking about? I am worried about my family." Sam gave up lying down and got out the bed. She padded toward the kitchen in search of a cup of coffee.

"If you did, then you would know Dad has cancer. He has a tumor, and it's inoperable."

The bombshell delivered stopped Sam dead in her tracks. "What?"

"Now that I have your attention, I'll ask again. What time shall we expect you home for the party?"

The wind had been knocked out of her. She struggled to speak. "I'll be there bright and early."

"Good and don't call Mom and stress her out any more than need be. She needs to remain strong for him. I'll see you next week."

The phone went dead.

"Ugh." The words had their intended affect. She was wide awake now. Sam slumped in a chair and allowed the tears to flow. That was so Tracey. When unable to get her way, she always resorted to dirty tactics. Tracey living near their parents didn't make Sam the bad child. She wanted a life, deserved a life, and went and sought one out.

She had no idea how long she stayed at the table before finally slow dragging herself to the shower. Sick dad or not, she had a case to solve first. Being undercover meant you stayed until the job was completed, or you were pulled off the case. Those dead girls' murderer needed to be caught. Her dad, of all people, would understand. He'd always been the main person to push and encourage her to stand up for what was right. In this moment, what was right was allowing these women's souls to be at peace with the bastard locked in a cell for life.

Vincent rolled his car to a stop at the entrance of the alley. His instincts had kicked in, and once again, he found himself retracing the steps of a killer, long after the crime scene had been trampled over.

Amber, just like Jasmine, had been found in an alley. The only difference was Mr. X didn't bother putting her in a dumpster located at the other end. What was it about this spot? He pulled up the crime scene photo on his tablet. Minus the torture, it looked as if she'd just slumped to the ground. Her knees were bent, and her left arm flailed out.

He flipped back to the other photos. There was a theme.

"Holy crap!" He snatched out his phone and dialed.

"What can I do for you?" the cheery voice of the White Rabbit answered. Knowing he was on the case left her without fear.

"Can you pull up the downtown area and plot all the locations in which the murders occurred?"

From the crime scene positions it looked as if Mr. X was marking his territory. Once the White Rabbit finished he'd know for sure.

"Sure thing." Clacking of fingers across a keyboard spilled through the line. "Done."

"Now connect them." He turned, looking out away from where the body would have been.

More clacking. "Got it."

"And send..."

"Already done."

The white envelope popped up on his tablet. He clicked on it and wondered how in the world the girl moved so fast. His eyes widened at the screen. X marks the spot, sort of. No murder occurred in the center so it was more of Mr. X leaving a big signature as he so often did at the crime scenes. “Thanks.”

“No problem. Hey, if you ever decide to go back in this full time, I’m your girl.” She giggled before ending the call.

He looked at the photo again. “What are you pointing to?”

The stretched out arm provided no solace, only leaving him with his thoughts.

Chapter 10

Sam watched groups of people walk up and down the sidewalk as she sat drinking her sweet tea on the patio of a small café. The only remains of her grilled turkey and bacon sandwich were the crumbs scattered about her plate. Anyone of the passersby could have murdered someone that morning and nobody would be the wiser.

"It seems like forever since we did this." Kara's voice pulled Sam's mind off the case and her father for a split second.

"Yes, it has."

"What's wrong?"

"My dad has cancer."

Kara's mouth dropped. "I'm so sorry. When are you going to see him?"

Sam shrugged. The thought of not being there now weighed on her.

"Work?" Kara gave her a knowing nod. She placed her hand on her friend's. "He'll understand. He's your number one supporter."

"You're right, but still." If not for the case, she'd be on the road already and she'd never of known of Vincent's return to the city. She had to know. "How long has your brother been back?"

Kara pulled her hand back. "What? How? When did you see him?"

"Did you or didn't you know?"

"I've seen him once. It was a few months ago. He seemed different and not at all happy to see me."

Sam frowned. "He's your brother, of course he was happy to see you."

"You didn't see his face. He walked out of my parents' house and just didn't want to be bothered."

"Have you tried reaching out to him since then?" She dug in her wallet and pulled out cash for the bill the waitress politely laid on the table. The woman had been very gracious while going about her duties since they arrived. Not once had she interrupted them.

"Of course and his response is he needs time to sort through some things. I have no idea what those things are of course."

"So why didn't you tell me you saw him?"

"And say what exactly. 'Hey, Sam, the love of your life is back in town and he doesn't want to be bothered?'" Her serious look turned into a smile.

Sam laughed. "He's never been the love of my life."

"Whatever. You've always been smitten with my brother."

Now that she couldn't argue. Her young heart knew exactly where it wanted to be. She just never wanted to compete with the long line of other women swooning over him, and she was way too young in high school. "You're lucky I have to get ready for work. Otherwise I'd give you a long list of reasons of why you are so wrong."

"Yeah, right."

They gave each other hugs, and Sam went on her way. Whatever Vincent's reasons were for not wanting family around had to be huge, but why request her for going undercover? He was a complicated man.

Sam wheeled her car into her apartments parking garage. She needed fresh outfits to wear that night. Her shoes echoed around the hall as her feet moved forward across the wooden floor. It would be just her luck if her neighbor across the hall came out. The old woman was friendly and very nosey.

No door creaking open. She made it to hers without incident. Her feet crumpled on top of something. She glanced down to see an oversized envelope. Someone had left her a package.

Sam cracked it open and pulled out the pictures. Her stomach turned. She'd just seen the girl the night before. Now her face was completely disfigured and almost distorted. If not for the tribal tattoo on her arm, she'd be unrecognizable unless by dental records.

She whipped out her phone and made a call.

"Captain?"

"I'm in the thick of this. I had the pictures delivered to you. We need to find out who this asshole is and stop him. Now! I don't care what you have to do. Somebody knows something."

She swallowed hard. "I think I can get more info." This left her with no choice concerning the parties. There was more going on behind the scenes, and she needed her ears to the ground no matter where the road led.

"Then get on it." The line went dead.

Sam grabbed her stuff and headed out. Leaving now gave her enough time to have a few moments to speak with Vincent before the rest of security and the girls rolled in. How in the world had another girl come up missing? The guys were extra vigilant and walked the girls out each night.

Once back at the club, she rushed inside, almost running to Vincent's office. She slowed herself as she neared and overheard voices.

"Are you sure it's Natalie?" Erica's voice cracked.

"Yes," Vincent replied. "It's no denying her tattoo."

"I can't believe this. Why my girls?"

"Can you think of any reason someone would be trying to send a message to you?"

"Are you serious? In this business? People protested my doors opening from the very beginning. But why my girls? Why not me if I'm the person they have an issue with?" Her voice sounded strained.

"I'm not even sure that's the problem. Right now, we need to be open to all possibilities. You'd be surprised at what motivates a person to kill." Sam marveled at Vincent's ability to maintain his composure.

"This bastard needs to be caught. If this keeps up, I won't have any girls left and I'm not sure if I can handle another funeral. Some of their parents don't even know where they work. To find out like this…"

"We're going to catch him."

Sam took that as her cue and tapped on the door gently so it wouldn't push open any farther.

Vincent pulled it open and welcomed her in. This time, he made sure to push the door until it latched. "Just the woman I'm looking for."

"Hey." She gave Erica a nod. "I didn't mean to interrupt."

Her glassy eyes gazed at Sam. "Not a problem. I'll let you two get down to business." She excused herself from the room.

Sam waited a moment before speaking. "Vincent, I received some photos. The captain had someone slide a package under my door."

"I've seen the latest."

She cocked her head at him. How in the world did he have the crime scene photos already? Yes, it's possible to have contacts on the force, but the girl was only found that morning.

"I have my ways."

"I'm impressed. I think I need to attend the 'private parties.'" The latter part fell out her mouth before she even registered what she'd said. No matter, it's what she needed to do.

Vincent picked up a tablet from off his desk. In a swift motion, he pulled up something on the screen. "Great. It will narrow down some of our suspects. The ME set time of death around three in the morning. That means she couldn't have been at the party longer than an hour, if she even attended at all."

Sam looked on in awe. The paperwork she received had no such information. She'd never met anyone as tuned into a case as he. Surely not Hastings, who spent more time selecting the right outfit than caring to delve into anything that would be considered work.

"Just before the evening ends, you need to be in my office. I will get you ready for tonight. You won't be going in without me listening and watching in every step of the way." He tapped on his device. "You're undercover and will need backup. I'm your support."

She'd seen plenty of movies and pat downs were common knowledge. "How do you suggest I hide a wire?"

"Let me worry about that. Go ahead and get ready for the shift. I'll see you back in here at 12:45, okay?"

She took the okay as more of her agreeing than asking if she were okay. He'd been a detective so she had no problems stepping back and allowing him to take the lead. Besides, having Vincent nearby would ease her nerves. "I'll see you then."

Vincent wasted no time getting things set up. His first call was to the White Rabbit. There was no one else he trusted in his home. She'd already bypassed his security system a few years earlier and didn't touch a thing, so why not? He needed high tech equipment and fast, not the police or military issued but the CIA stuff.

Afterward, he focused on the club. Erica thought it best not to bring up Natalie unless asked directly. Most girls didn't watch the news, making the chances slim.

Like clockwork, he met with his guys and set up his station just as the girls filtered out from the back and morphed into almost every man's fantasy. Sam was no exception. The red and black leopard mini dress hugged her curves in all the right places as she strolled by him. Her legs were no longer wobbly in the stilettos but not quite at gazelle status yet. Her toned thighs extended out and covered the room, and she blended in with the other models.

Vincent glanced up and noticed another male watching Sam. Seeing the flashy suit in the building made his blood boil. What the hell did Hastings want? His outfit looked more of a drug lord than a lead detective. The man had been that way from the day he left the uniform behind.

He approached Hastings. "Can I help you, detective?"

Hastings frowned. Vincent couldn't blame him. Observing Sam this way had him looking as well. No matter, he needed to do whatever it was he came in for and leave.

"I need to have a word with Sam." He gave Vincent the once over, and his right cheek moved up in a sly grin. "Nice outfit. It suits you."

"I can't say so much for yours." Vincent leaned in and lowered his voice. "This isn't the best place for you to talk to her."

"Is that so? I can speak with her wherever I damn well please."

"Rule number one on being undercover. Avoid known cops, detective." He raised his voice and waved to Jenna. Vincent would make sure he had no chance in speaking with Sam now. "Get the good detective here anything he wants on the house."

"Sure thing." A fake smile spread across Jenna's lips.

Vincent spoke under his breath. "We wouldn't want her cover blown now, would we? What the hell are you thinking?"

"Tell her she needs to check in as soon as she gets off."

"That's when check ins are…off duty." Vincent didn't buy the check-in line. Hastings wanted to get a peek at Sam, simple as that. There was nothing wrong with her cell phone to notify her for a check-in. Those were set up prior to going undercover and Hastings knew better. How in the world did Sam get involved with the likes of him? No time to ponder it. One of the girls had a client ready for the back. He covered the short distance and posted at his station.

Time went in slow motion as he waited for Sam to get a show. He needed to know if they'd be any after hour's party tonight. With the flick of his wrist, another card was approved on the credit card machine but not before catching the name. He'd made mental notes of all the name's to run checks on them in his off hours. The process had him up early in the morning and he'd come up empty so far. Out of the corner of his eye, he saw a young Asian girl bopping his way.

"Enjoy your show," he said to the couple and quickly buzzed them in.

"Hey." The girl stopped in front of his table. She wore a black and grey bustier, black leggings, and Doc Martins. Her semi-gothic outfit was a contrast to the half-naked woman he allowed behind the door.

"What are you doing in here?" Vincent was pleasantly surprised to see his young hacker friend.

"Getting out of my rabbit hole." She glanced around. "Besides, I wanted to know what it actually looks like on the inside. I'm old enough now." Age was relative compared to how old she actually looked. Her small stature barely made her to be fourteen. Even with the thick heels on her boots, she still barely reached five feet two inches. "So this is what you do for a living. Sweet." Her head bobbed, and a huge grin plastered across her face.

"I asked you to text me. I would have come outside."

"And miss out on the fun?" She placed a small bag of items on the stand. "So when are we doing this thing?"

"What thing?"

She raised a pierced eyebrow at him. "The thing that requires earpieces and hidden cameras. I'm in."

He shook his head. "No, you're my computer geek. My go to girl."

"Ah, so you admit that you need my skills. Thanks, partner." She winked at him and walked off. Her small stature faded into the crowd as she got farther away.

Moments later, he received a text.

White Rabbit: No worries I'm gone. I can't compete with the fake T&A.

It was followed by a smiley face.

Vincent shook his head and got back to work. An hour and a half passed, and it was time to shut his station down. No more back room action after 12:45 on a weekday.

As instructed, Sam was headed in his direction. His mind raced with ideas of what she could have possible said to shake her company. The guy had been glued to her all night and had paid generously for her time. It didn't happen often, but there were a few guys who were too embarrassed to go to the back so they paid the girls just to spend time with them in V.I.P.

He buzzed her in and then switched the latch to stay open for the other models to shut it down for the night before heading to his office. Sam leaned against the wall to his office. Her body slouched and one leg extended out, resting her foot on its heel. Instead of the beautiful smile she'd displayed most of the night, her face lay slack as her head rested against the wall.

"Skylar gave me the go ahead and an address and time to show up at."

"Come on in and have a seat." He needed her to get as much rest in as possible.

"You really think we'll catch this guy?"

"I do. The problem is whether it will be before he kills again. Are you sure you're up to this?"

She stifled a yawn and nodded.

"Good." She needed to be. Mr. X had played this game far too long and this wouldn't be easy. He resisted the urge to pull her into his arms. "Come on let's get you ready."

Chapter 11

Sam's breathing slowed when Skylar tapped on the door to the house. She didn't know what to expect on the other side and braced herself for anything and everything.

A small mail-sized slot opened just above their heads. Eyes appeared, giving them the once over. It slid shut, and the door opened. Music played in the background as people lounged about or remained standing as they talked in groups or coupled up. Not the orgy she expected. If not for the girls prancing around in lingerie, it could have been any sort of gathering.

"Wow, this is nice," she said, more to let Vincent know than to Skylar. When they approached the house, it was hard for her not to look around and see which vehicle Vincent would be in as he monitored her from a distance.

Skylar's long legs guided them to a couch. She unbuttoned the thin brown jacket she wore and let it fall to the sofa. Perky breasts and flat abs squeezed into a floral lace bodice and panties were on full display. Eager eyes rolled toward her. She smiled at Sam.

My turn? Sam fumbled with the zipper but somehow managed to pull it down. Her attempt to be like Skylar and allow the jacket to fall gracefully on the couch came off flat. It fell to a heap on the floor instead. Skylar swooped it up and tossed it on the upholstery for Sam.

"I can see you very clear now," Vincent spoke in her ear. "I wondered how long you were going to keep the jacket on."

"Whatever," she mumbled.

"Don't break character. Be nice and I'll meet you at your place after."

My place? Clothes tossed about and unwashed dishes flooded her mind. Did she remember to throw away yesterday's Chinese food? "No. I'll come to yours."

She'd save the rest of her words for later. Nothing was easy about wearing this lace chemise in front of a room full of people. Especially the men. She felt like the manager's special at a supermarket. Everyone needed to have a look. It didn't help that the outfit she wore was Vincent's choice. He insisted the camera would fit inside the small faux glass buttons better. That may be so, but it left her feeling a little breezy. It was something she'd never wear on the main floor of Pleasures' but probably would in the backroom when her time had been purchased.

Sam smoothed down the front of her outfit and eased down on the couch. Her back straight, chest up, and legs crossed, she leaned back into the soft cushions. She said sat? poised, the move taken from her mother's unsuccessful attempt at sending her to a few charm classes.

Fingers ran through her hair as she tried to look unassuming while scoping out the room. A sultry redhead in green gripped the edge of a necktie and led a wide-eyed man up a set of stairs. Two girls toyed with a gentleman sitting in a lounge chair. Their gangly arms grazed up and down his body as they whispered in his ear. His eyes rolled back in pleasure. More whispers, and they too found themselves heading up the stairs.

"I take it the upstairs is where the fun is."

Skylar paid her no mind. She, too, was busy flirting away with a gentleman who seemed enthralled with the lace of her outfit. His hands outlined the edge of the thin material. She giggled, allowing him to continue, and stood, chatting with him for his full attention.

No matter. Sam's words were for the man in her ear. It was her way of letting him know that there was action happening there.

"You look amazing." She was graced with a smile from a salt and peppered hair man.

A sense of familiarity washed over her as she glanced up at him. He wasn't tall in stature but his presence commanded attention. The room was full of expensive business suits and watches, nothing but Atlanta's elite. He along with everyone in there oozed with money. But him, she'd seen somewhere before. "Thank you."

"This must be your first time." Gentle eyes smiled at her. She didn't fall for them. The looks may be kind, but he still was there searching for a party girl.

"It is." She played along by batting her mascara painted lashes at him.

"Allow me to show you the ropes then. I'm Gerald."

She smiled, but her gaze went past him to Skylar.

Skylar took the hint and came over. “One second, Gerald. I need to have a girl moment with my friend.” She tousled his hair.

“No problem,” he growled. “Make it quick though.”

She stepped off to the side with Sam and whispered in her ear, “We receive the money by courier in the morning.”

“But how will they know where to deliver it?” She had no intentions on giving up her personal information.

“No worries. I wouldn’t have asked you to come if you hadn’t already been checked out. They know where to come.”

Panic started to set in.

“Relax, *chica*. They don’t ever come inside. It’s just dropped in your mailbox. Now, go be nice for Gerald. He’s easy for your first time. He only likes to watch.” Skylar gave her a peck on the cheek and quickly made her way back to her gentleman of the evening.

“What the hell is going on?” she mumbled.

“Don’t worry. I figured there’d be someone checking you out. The captain did a great job with your fake information. The address they checked on was the same one listed on the application Erica put on file for you. It’s to one of her condos’. I’ve swung by a few times and turned on the lights to make it seem like someone’s there from time to time.” Vincent’s calm voice settled her nerves a bit.

She moved closer to the man.

“So, are we all set?” Gerald grinned at her.

“Yes, I’m good.”

“Good. Let’s go upstairs, shall we?”

A lump formed in her throat.

"Skylar said he only likes to watch. I don't think she'll set you up," Vincent answered.

"Sure, why not?" She looped her arm around Gerald and let him guide her away from everyone.

———

Vincent nudged the White Rabbit again for giggling. They sat on a side bench in the back of the van with their eyes glued to laptops and tablets. The White Rabbit streamed video as well as running facial analysis.

"What?" She shrugged. "Are you watching the look on this guy's face? He probably just jizzed in his pants."

"Jiz?"

"Come on. You work in the adult industry and don't know what jiz is?" Her face turned into a mock. "Ejaculation."

"I don't care to know about another man's fluids. Did you get the last one?" The quick scan of the room Sam did for them worked out wonderful. In minutes all of their faces had been captured. The camera on the outside of the van captured them as they left. Vincent will be able run checks on them.

"Yes."

"Good. This way they'll be no doubt on what girl was with what guy when they left either."

"Well, your friend is about to find out. By the way, I saw her in the club. She's gorgeous. It's hard to believe she's a cop. I remembered her picture from the initial hacking I did," she babbled on, chattering nonstop like the eighteen-year-old she was. "When are you going to ask her out?"

"Quiet. They're going in the room." Vincent cursed on the inside for the hundredth time for encouraging Sam to go to the place. Another for extra measure for when the White Rabbit stepped in front of his undercover vehicle as he was getting ready to pull off from the storage place. She had insisted on coming and wouldn't move her motorcycle until he gave in.

"Have a seat on the bench," Gerald's voice filtered into the earpiece.

Their view of the room lowered as Sam complied.

Gerald perched himself on the edge of a bed. "Show me how you please yourself."

Sam coughed.

"I will stay over here. Go ahead. Let me see you. I know you get naked in the club so what's the difference?"

The camera fumbled around, obstructing their view before focusing again. Sam had positioned her outfit back on Gerald.

"Your breasts are amazing!" Gerald flashed his tongue.

Vincent winced.

"Rub them."

"Like this?" Sam whispered.

"Yes! Yes! Rub them for big daddy." Gerald's hand went down his pants. "Put your hand on that cunt and rub it for me, baby."

"Like this?"

"Yes! Rub and show me how much you like it." His eyes rolled to the back of his head.

"Great, I'm watching a porno." Vincent put his hand over his face.

The White Rabbit giggled again. "This is awesome."

"I love it, big daddy!" Sam screamed.

"Oh God!" Gerald's body jerked.

"See. Jiz in the pants."

Vincent nudged his unwanted guest again.

She laughed.

"Was it good for you?" Sam asked.

"Is she talking to you or him? It's obvious that loser enjoyed. That's Judge Gerald Kapenski, by the way. I just got a facial recognition match." The excitement over, White Rabbit pushed her glassed up on her face and pecked away.

"I knew he looked familiar." He clicked on the earpiece. "Sam, I think we have enough for the night. I'm going to run checks on them as soon as we leave. If anything happens to one of the girls we have video of the man they left with. Thank him and get hell out of there. Several people have already left. They are off to other locations, and I don't want you anywhere in that action."

"Thank you so much, Gerald," Sam purred.

"No." He gulped through breaths. "Thank you."

"How much you want to bet he goes downstairs and shakes hands with the jizzy hand?" the White Rabbit joked.

"Dammit! You're putting images in my head that I don't want to even think about." He clicked the earpiece again. "Sam, just go."

"I'll see you next time, Gerald." Her voice was sensual, more so than her usual pretend voice.

Vincent remained silent until Sam stepped foot back outside. Gerald appeared right on her heels and escorted her to her car. "The perfect gentleman after paying for a prostitute, the irony of it. I'm going to follow for a few blocks just to make sure he doesn't get other ideas." He moved to the driver seat of the van.

His partner began closing down shop and hopped in the front seat.

"Sam."

"Yes." The sound of her engine roared to life.

"Take an alternate route. I want to make sure this jerk isn't following you."

"Okay."

He paused at her tone. Sam was a little happy to have just walked out of that situation. "Are you okay?"

"I'm fine. See you at your place for the debriefing." The low volume of music turned up in his ear.

Vincent kept his distance from Sam, close enough to see everything but not so close to scare anyone away. After a while, he was satisfied that she wasn't being followed. He made a quick detour and dropped the White Rabbit off then sped home to Sam. Listening to her with Gerald caused his temperate to rise.

Chapter 12

Vincent stood in his foyer with his mouth wide open. The trench coat Sam wore glided to the floor. Her womanly curves, barely covered by the lacey material, were more magnificent in person than watching on a monitor. He'd just calmed himself down and now this. Have mercy. She was torturing him.

Her eyes were filled with lust. He didn't have time to register what was happening when her lips found his. His head spun, and the kiss deepened. He allowed her all the access to his mouth that she—no he'd be a fool to put it all on her—he needed.

From the moment she'd turned eighteen, he knew the pull he felt toward the young, brown-eyed girl wasn't just the brotherly affection he felt toward his own sister. Many nights, he'd slept with a rise in his boxers thinking about her only a few doors away in his sister's room. Even when he'd left for the academy, his thoughts never strayed too far. Of course there'd been other women, but none ever pulled at his soul like Sam.

Fingers intertwining in the back of her hair, he gently tugged on the base of her head and pulled her closer.

Her heartbeat riveted through his chest as he slowly walked her to the couch.

Sam pushed him back into the leather and climbed on top. She obviously wasn't in the mood for taking their time. She yanked on his shirt, tugging it up until he sat bare chested.

His breath caught in his throat when her tongue snaked out and flicked across his muscles. She outlined the ridge of his pectorals, sending a tingling sensation down his spine. He palmed her back with one hand, and the other found the small metal clasp holding her bra in place. In a quick motion, he unlatched it, setting her taut breast freed. Even without silicone enhancements, they sat up perfect.

Vincent trailed a finger around her brown areolas, marveling in the complexity of it. The brown peek beckoned to him, and he obliged. His mouth sought them out. The first taste was sweeter than the freshest honeydew on a summer morning.

"Mmm." Her soft moan caught him off guard. His excitement elevated to another level.

Vincent let out a growl as he moved to the side of the couch. He couldn't bear not to touch her any longer.

His hand shook as he moved it up the inside of her thigh. Their eyes met, and he drifted into their deep caverns. She nodded and lifted her hips, allowing for the removal of her lace panties. He gently slid them down, his hand drifting dangerously closer to her moist center. Vincent could smell her sex, and the scent was driving him insane. All he wanted to do was thrust deep into her and fulfill every fantasy he'd ever had, but he knew he had to control the need. This could be their one and only chance.

Vincent wanted to savor this moment in case he never received another opportunity. The dilation of her pupils hadn't been missed. Sam was on a high, fueled by adrenaline. Not able to hold off any longer, he tested her center by inserting a finger. A groan filled the air, and Vincent wasn't sure which of them had uttered it. His eyes rolled back. For just a moment longer, he allowed himself the pleasure of feeling her wetness around the tip before inching it in deeper. This time he knew for sure the animal sound that filled the air was from him.

"Vincent."

His eyes snapped open, and he gazed up at her.

"I need you," she whispered. "My body's on fire. I have to feel you."

Waves of emotions washed over him at her softly spoken words. So many things he wanted to say, yet none of them could make it pass the lump in his throat. Instead, he laid his head against her chest, savoring the moment. Her heart raced against him. His inner torment soon to be relieved, he raised his head and allowed their gazes to meet again.

"I'm all yours," he managed to murmured before taking her mouth.

All the emotions and feelings he'd harbored over the years came out. His tongue brushed against her closed lips, and she eagerly opened for him. Their moans mingled as their kiss deepened.

Sam reached over and grabbed a handful of his hair, tugging him closer to her. The pain of her grip in his tresses was a welcome thing as she pulled him to the side. Sam maneuvered him on top and busied herself with unfastening his pants and pushing them down. He helped when they reached below his hips, yanking them off and let them fall to the floor next to the couch.

She spread her legs wide to accommodate him. They fastened tightly around him, causing his manhood to brush against her nub. Her body rocked against his, sending waves of pleasure throughout both of them.

"I need you in me badly," she moaned, her voice raspy against his ear.

Her tongue licked his ear lobe before gently nibbling on it. A shiver ran up his spine. He fought the urge to thrust into her heat and give them both what they wanted. He lifted his body away from hers as much as he could with the grip she had around his waist.

As bad as he wanted to enter her, he hesitated. "Sam," he began. "I need to get a condom."

"No talking. I want you to take me. Now!" She pulled his head down to hers for a kiss.

She ran her tongue across his teeth before opening her mouth to deepen their joining. Her hand inched down and traced the rim of his pride before running a fingertip up and down the full length of him. She broke off their kiss and lowered her head in amazement.

"You're huge," she said almost to herself.

Vincent's chest swelled with pride. It wasn't the first time he had heard those words, but it was different coming from her. When her thumb brushed across the tip again, he couldn't keep his groan of pleasure at bay. He wanted to beg her to taste him. Her mouth was open, and it was so close. A little farther and she could wrap those lips around him.

Her attention went to the floor. "Got it." She held up a condom. It fell out my bra.

Vincent took it from her and ripped it open. Her eyes were on him while he rolled it on.

The fire shining in her brown gaze was almost too much for him. How long had he waited to see that look from her? Vincent sent up a silent prayer he could make this good for her.

His tongue thrust deeply into the cavern of her mouth at the same time he thrust deeply into her welcoming body.

She tore her mouth away from his. "Ah, shit."

Afraid he'd hurt her, he started to pull away, but her legs tightened around him, keeping him where he was. He stayed still, afraid to move.

"Are you okay?"

Her eyes fluttered open. "Yes. Take me. I'm yours." She rejoined her mouth with his.

It was all the encouragement he needed. He pulled out of her and reentered slowly, ensuring he felt every inch of her and she him. For long moments, he teased them both until he didn't know if he could stand it any longer. His balls tightened against his body, and his rod stiffened. A thin layer of sweat formed against his brow as he fought to hold onto his control.

He pulled back out her moisture. "I don't know how much longer I can hold out," he said between his clenched teeth.

"Who asked you to?"

The challenge was clear. Desire burned deep within her eyes. It was all the invitation he needed. He dove into her. Long slow strokes were replaced with hard short pounding thrusts. Her fingers gripped his back. Sam's fingernails sank into his skin as she thrust upward to meet his motions. He knew he would be bruised tomorrow, but it didn't matter. Just like he cared less about the bite mark he was sure to have on his chest from the gnawing of her teeth against him. None of it mattered. It would be a reminder for him that tonight had happened and it hadn't been a part of his overactive imagination. She'd yearned for him as much as he for her.

"Oh, Vincent, I'm so close. Harder," Sam breathed against his ear before giving it a soft tug.

The slight pain nudged him on, and he began to thrust in and out of her faster and harder. When his shaft hit her back walls, he knew he wouldn't be able to hold on to the orgasm tingling at the base of his spine.

"I can't hold off any longer, Sam." His words brushed against her neck.

He felt it moving up the base of his rod. His testicles stiffened against his body. The first wave caught him off guard, and he gasped for breath. His orgasm was so powerful Vincent could barely breathe as he continued to move into her. Her muscles tightened around him, and she began to quiver beneath him.

Together, they reached their peak. The quiet of the room was only disturbed by the harsh sounds of their breathing as they each attempted to catch their breath. He glanced down at the woman beneath him, her eyes closed, a soft smile on her lips. He brushed the hair away from her damp forehead. All the years he'd watched and waited, praying for his chance. Their joining had exceeded all his expectations.

But then, reality began to set in. Vincent said, "You know, relationships built off adrenaline rushes rarely last."

"I guess we need to keep the adrenaline flowing then." She stifled a yawn and moved her body closer to his, nuzzling against his chest.

Soon, Sam's breathing deepened, and she rested beneath him. He planted a small kiss on her forehead and allowed her the moment of rest. This was exactly what he'd needed. How long had it been since he'd relaxed? Too long and this wasn't the time either.

Vincent waited until she drifted off and then went to work. Within an hour he'd had background on everyone at the party. Including the man who'd put the whole thing on. But, it was the man beside him that interested Vincent more—the Hungarian's brother Sebestyen. On the video he could be seen having disagreements with several of the girls.

Satisfied with his progress, he allowed himself to enjoy the moment. He returned to Sam and took her in his arms once again. Tomorrow he'd do more digging into Sebestyen.

Chapter 13

Sam jerked awake with a start. Darkness enveloped her, and something held her body down. She blinked, and her eyes adjusted to Vincent lying next to her, his arm draped across her waist.

She was in a room, Vincent's room to be exact. The hours before pounded against her mind. She'd been in control the first round, but the second, which landed them in his bed, had been all him. Vincent had taken her like no other. A smile spread across her face.

"You awake?" His voice was groggy.

"Yes."

"You want to talk about…"

"What we did was amazing, don't ruin it. I know this doesn't constitute a relationship, but let's enjoy the moments we share." No need to rehash everything. She'd put herself out there, and he'd accepted. The only way she'd been able to pretend for the guy was imagining Vincent touching her. It had turned her on way more than she anticipated.

He didn't need to bother with the gentle let down and send her on the walk of shame. She sat up and pulled the cover with her in her search to find clothing. Reality hit her. She didn't have clothing. All she had were the skimpy underwear she'd kept on from the party.

"The case."

"Oh." She gripped the material around her. It didn't matter that he'd already explored every inch of her. Being next to him like this left her feeling exposed. "Can I get a t-shirt or something?"

"You know how long I've waited to see you like this?" A sly grin spread across his face, and he hesitated.

She narrowed her eyes at him. *What did he just say? He's been wanting to see me like this?* Soon as she put on clothes, they needed to discuss this.

"Sure." He tossed the cover off and walked to the closet.

Goodness, even his ass is perfect. She licked her dry lips as he sauntered past.

He returned, wearing gym shorts and a wife beater. The look caught her off guard. If not for his skin tone, his style of dress could have passed for the same thing many of the boys in her patrol area wore. Amazing how perception was everything. The majority of people would cross the street when seeing the teens she saw every day at work but wouldn't give Vincent a second thought of being threatening.

He handed her a shirt and a pair of jogging pants. Sam gave him a sideways glance at the small size and pink lettering. No way in hell would she put on one of his other women's clothing. For all she knew, it could be one of the girls from the club. Other men couldn't resist them. What would make Vincent so different?

"The outfit is Kara's. I've had it for years. She left it at my apartment while I was on the force. You remember how close I lived to the gym she worked out at?"

Oh, yes. She did remember. Her jealousy subsided a bit. She accepted the clothing. "Thank you."

"I'm going to head down and make us something to eat while you get dressed." He disappeared out of the room.

She took her time and washed up in the master bathroom. Kara's outfit was a little big, due to her extremely long arms and legs. Sam cuffed the wrists and folded the pants at the waist for adjustment. Happy with the results, she made her way downstairs.

The smell of food sailed up and into her senses. Vincent scooped up items out a skillet resting on his flat range stove and put them on a plate. Sam smiled when he sat it in front of her. Chicken sausage patties and egg whites cooked to perfection rested on the dish. "Looks delicious." What else did this man know how to do?

He turned and removed a cup from an expensive coffee maker, or at least that's what she assumed it was. It looked more high tech than any she'd ever seen.

"It must be nice to have a trust fund."

Vincent looked embarrassed as he placed the cup on the counter.

"What made you ever want to be a cop, or a security guard for that matter? It's obvious you don't need the money. Hell, that gadget alone is a half months pay for me, probably more. I'd have to choose, great coffee or being served an eviction notice." She laughed and took a sip off the best coffee she'd ever experienced. Skip Starbucks. She'd come to Vincent's house and gladly pay.

"You know my mom died when I was a teen, right?" His facial expression went from embarrassed to serious.

She nodded. "I never knew what happened. Kara never spoke of it." The questions about him wanting to see her naked would have to wait. This was proprietary information, and she was all ears.

"It's because she never knew the true story. For Kara, some punk robbed our mother and killed her. Nothing could be further from the truth." Vincent's gaze saddened, and he drifted off to somewhere as he continued speaking. "I was home the first time the police came with the news."

Sam listened. Tuned into his vulnerably, she knew this wasn't easy for him. Vincent had his pride and she wouldn't push.

Vincent swallowed hard. This was the first time he'd ever allowed the full story to fall from his lips. "My mother was murdered in Reynoldstown by Mr. X."

"What?" Her mouth dropped open. Like Vincent, she, too, knew the history of Mr. X. "I thought he only went after working girls."

His brows knit together..

"Oh my God!" Hands flew to her mouth.

"Yes. My mother was a prostitute. My world shattered when I found out. But what I discovered while as a cop was ten times worse."

Her eyes widened in disbelief.

"I investigated a case while as a detective and uncovered that the people I looked into had shady dealings. They'd given out a lot of loans but at steep price. A price so high, that if you didn't pay your debts the Mafia would be ashamed of how you'd be dealt with. I saw my dad's name listed on the books during the bust." He ran his fingers through his hair, pausing a moment before dropping the bomb on her. "My dad owed a half a million from his gambling addiction. Apparently, my mom working as a prostitute was to cover his debts and help repay the money. If not, they would have killed him and still went after her for the money. My trust came from the insurance money. She wanted to make sure her kids were taken care of."

"But you guys lived so well. What about his business?"

"They got a piece of everything. They wouldn't ruin him. Otherwise they couldn't control him."

Sam rocked back on the barstool, her mouth agape.

"Exactly my first reaction. I confronted my dad about it, and he'd already beaten himself up enough. His words did little to help me understand though."

"Vincent. I'm so sorry."

"It's why I left the force and disappeared for a while. I had to sort out some things."

Her eyes saddened in understanding.

"I have to catch this guy." He began working on a touch screen computer built into the countertop. He'd recently had it installed, and from the look on Sam's face now, she was intrigued. The only thing more exciting than this new feature was what lay beneath her sweat pants. Below the extra layers resided a magnificent wonder and he'd enjoyed partaking in exploring every inch of it. His bulge stiffened at the idea of having her again.

"Who are you? Iron Man? Batman? What is this?" Her voice cut into his thoughts and steered him back on track.

"Trust fund money put to good use." His fingers whipped across the gadget. "These are photos from last night, thanks to the camera you wore. I ran a check on everyone in the room. Atlanta's Elite was definitely in the building." He did a movement with his hand, knocking the array of pictures out the way and enlarging one on the screen. "Except for this guy. This is Leonard Bartos from Hungary."

"I remember him. He didn't speak but only sat back and watched everyone. The girls seemed comfortable with him."

"They should be. He's the sponsor for the whole shindig. The building is in his mother's name. I did some research, and his brother lives in New York. There's no doubt in my mind that he's in charge of similar places there."

"Do you think this is our guy?" She studied the image.

"No. He'd never get his hands dirty and why ruin his business? Dead girls mean he loses out. I think Mr. X. is someone he's had dealings with."

"How do you want to handle it?"

"I already have someone following his every move as we speak." Vincent dropped the image down.

"What do I tell Hastings? I see he's been blowing up my phone all night."

Vincent scowled. *What the hell did that guy want in the middle of the night?* Whatever it was, surely it could wait. There hadn't been any new developments. The White

Rabbit was monitoring the precinct's every move by skillfully hacking into their system and the cameras. He'd be updated at the same time they were.

"Nothing," he replied. Hastings was the reason for the flub the first time around. He'd been too busy parading for cameras and locked up the wrong guy, though the asshole would never admit it. "He doesn't need to know about the house. If so, then he'd be too busy trying to raid it before we got our man. This needs a more subtle approach."

"I agree. There's nothing subtle about Hastings. I'll check in but hold back until we have something more concrete."

Her words held a double meaning of which Vincent didn't want to get into. Sam was an adult, and they all make mistakes. He'll just assume Hastings was one since they're no longer together. "We're close. I can feel it."

Sam leaned into him, and they continued studying the photos. Vincent kept his concentration but lavished the closeness. He couldn't wait for the case to be over to learn more about the beautiful woman she'd become.

Chapter 14

Vincent eased down in his seat, careful that Sebestyen couldn't see him as he crossed the street. This was the third place he'd followed him to. The guy crossed the street and marched up to a door. He banged on it. The metal of the screen door frame rattled into Vincent's cracked window.

A red head answered. Vincent zoomed his camera in for a closer view. The woman didn't work for Pleasures but she defiantly worked in the adult industry. Her open rob, a testament that she had no issue showing off her body.

Vincent adjusted the sound on his listening device.

"I already told you I'm no longer doing calls. I'm not into that anymore," the woman's tone cracked in aggravation.

He gripped her arm. "You won't stop until I tell you to. Be there tonight or else." His accent thick but Vincent still could make out the words.

"Or else what?"

"You don't want to know." He released her arm and walked away.

The woman slammed the door.

Vincent continued following Sebestyen until it was almost time for him to get to work for the evening.

Sam nearly floated from her car to the door of Pleasures. She'd been this way all day. Vincent was the perfect match for her sexually repressed drive.

"Walker!" The voice reached up like a hand and snatched her from off her cloud.

She turned and faced Hastings just before her hand reached the buzzer to the club. "Yes." Her cheeks protested the fake smile she gave him.

"Are you going to keep avoiding me?" He glared at her.

"I was told to report every forty-eight hours. It just now turned forty-six."

"This isn't about the case, and you know it. Man," he gave her a good once over, "you look great."

"And you're still the same."

"Come on, Sam. Things happen."

"Like only being with me when it suits you? I'm not some toy. Go away and tell Barnes hello for me." She'd had her suspicions, and from his uncomfortable facial expression, she'd been right. "Leave before you blow my cover. Don't call me unless there's been a development, and I'll do the same."

She pressed down on the buzzer. Vincent immediately opened the door. He'd no doubt watched the whole thing from behind the one-way window. She stepped in and allowed the door to close without a backward glance.

"You okay?" Vincent searched her face for answers.

"I'm fine. Seeing you again just made it all better." She fell into his arms for an embrace.

"Same here. It's time for my meeting with the guys. I'll see you later." He paused before giving her a kiss on the forehead.

She blushed as he walked off. Sam took her time following behind. She needed to wait until the rosiness she no doubt had on her face faded away before anyone saw her.

"Hey, Jenna," she said, passing the bar.

"Hey." She stacked some glasses. "What did you get into last night?"

"Nothing much," she lied. No way Jenna was in on the private party set up. Why would she be? She wasn't a dancer.

"Oh, okay. I just know some girls get together and go clubbing on Thursday evenings. Anyway, get ready because it's Friday and there's a whole different crowd in here. All the big ballers will be in here trying to outdo each other."

Sam laughed. "Thanks for the heads up."

"I'm just looking out. We girls have to stick together."

She couldn't agree more. Sam continued on to the locker room and changed into her evening attire. She'd fallen into a routine: clothes, hair, and then makeup. Afterward, they had their meeting. Erica didn't have much to say for once.

Transformed, Sam stepped from behind the back door. Her confidence had grown from the day before. She led the way as they all filtered out. Tonight, she planned to be bold and work the room. No need to sit back and let the men come to her. She needed to touch bases with as many as she could. Who all knew about the private parties, and furthermore who knew the Hungarian?

Jenna winked at her as Sam took a seat at the bar.

"Looking nice, lady," a male voice called over her shoulder.

Her lips puckered and ready, Sam turned around. "Hey there, hand…" Her words fell off as she registered a guy from the precinct.

"Wow, you're in full character," he said, his voice lowered. "The guys would not believe this. If I could get away with taking a picture, I would."

"What are you doing here, Johnson?" Sam adjusted her clothing as best as the skimpy outfit would allow.

"Hey, Mark! You buying my girl a drink or what?" Jenna shouted over the music.

Sam's eyebrow rose at the first name recognition.

"What do you want? Your usual? A bud?" he asked.

Sam rolled her eyes. "Malibu and sprite please."

"Coming up." Jenna tapped the bar with her skull ring when she spoke.

"Johnson, what are you doing here?" she whispered.

"Play along. Get the drink and we'll move to a corner."

Hastings' lackey being in the building squelched her confidence. It ran and jumped out the nearest window, and she wished she could follow.

Vincent spotted Johnson from the moment he'd walked in the front door. He'd gone straight to the bar and not after the girls as he'd done on previous visits. In fact, since Sam started working there, he hadn't seen the guy at all. Something was up.

His phone vibrated.

White Rabbit: *Update. You need to hear this now.*

He clicked on his headset. "Zack, I need you to cover the rooms for a moment."

"Gottcha," Zach came back. "On my way."

Moments later, Vincent gave Zack a nod and rushed to the security room for privacy. Phone in hand, he called the White Rabbit.

She negated saying hello and spilled the information with the excitement as if she'd just figured out the theory of relativity. "The police station is in an uproar. I've been monitoring them all morning. Some guy's fingerprints have been found at two of the girls' houses, and there's a witness who saw him leaving Natalie's apartment the night before her body turned up."

Vincent processed the information. "Any mention of who this man is?"

"Yes, Dr. Barnes. They're on their way to pick him up now."

That would explain why Johnson was there. "Okay. Keep monitoring them. I'll talk to Sam."

"No problem."

Vincent had no doubt Sam would be relieved and couldn't wait to get away from this place. His gut told him that they have the wrong guy once again. Dr. Barnes was a regular and frequented the same two girls at the club. Even at the private party he chose one of the same girls. Why turn around and kill one? It wouldn't matter though. Once Hastings got ahold of Dr. Barnes, he'd be like a dog with a bone and not let go. He ended the call and headed back toward the main area.

To his surprise, Sam was already in route to him. He picked up the pace and met her in the middle of the hall.

"One of the guy's from the precinct was here. Johnson." She wrung her hands together.

"I saw. I know him."

"They have a suspect. That's why he showed up."

"I've just got a heads up as well."

She gave an inquisitive glance and tilted her head to the side.

"I have my ways." He'd spare her the part about having the system hacked.

"The captain wants me there for the interrogation."

"He's right. You should be. Dr. Barnes was a regular here. You can provide them with more information." Vincent waited for one of the girl's to pass by and get out of ear shot before continuing, "I don't take him for our guy. Sure, he's a perv but no more than anyone else. It'll be pretty dumb to murder girls that this entire club has seen him with."

"I agree."

"I'll catch Erica and let her know. All the girls will think you had a family emergency. Get going." Vincent stepped to the side as Sam took off down the hall. With each step, her sultry stride she learned from the girls shed into her tomboyish walk. Her fingers went up and entwined with her hair pulling it into a ponytail. She slipped from dancer back to cop.

Moments later, Sam brushed past his post as he spoke with Zach. Her makeup was washed off as best as she could, she no longer looked like an entertainer but a very sexy woman nonetheless. Without a second glance, she made her exit from the club. Vincent wasn't long after. The case was more important than working tonight.

Back in his apartment, he watched the interrogation rooms, courtesy of his young gifted friend, and sorted through all the pictures she'd provided from trailing the Hungarian brother early that day. None of the people he visited raised a concern outside of the woman, Stacy Walter's. Come to find out she did try out for a spot at Pleasures but Erica didn't hire her. She found a home at another strip club. One that wasn't nearly as upscale.

He went back to crossing checking the people from the party making sure he didn't miss anything. Most didn't even live in Atlanta during the 90's. That was the problem with the city, everyone was a darn transplant. If they didn't reside in the city then how could they be Mr. X. There was no way the new killings were the works of a copycat. The signature never made it to the little bit of news coverage the case had.

His suspects were narrowed down to two people who did live in the city during the first murders—Dr. Barnes and Sebestyen. After what he witnessed earlier the scales tipped more for Sebestyen.

Raised voices on the streaming video caught his attention. He glanced at the monitor.

"I don't care what his wife says. This is our guy!" Hastings fussed at Sam. They stood behind the one-way mirror on the other side of interrogation room two.

The White Rabbit's release of the mute button in the room and gave Vincent the fly on the wall experience.

"All I'm saying is the guy is guilty of sleeping with prostitutes but not much else. His wife says he was home during the time the ME report says the time of death occurred." Sam crossed her arms in defense.

"And you've been a detective all of what? Two weeks?" Hastings smirked. "Everyone should just pull up a chair and listen, but then they'll remember that you aren't a detective at all. You just happened to be the lucky pick for going undercover."

Vincent wanted to deck the guy for Sam.

"Some things never change I see. Ignore the facts just so you can be right."

Vincent was proud of her for standing her ground but knew the outcome wouldn't be in her favor.

"The fact is the wife is a liar. Dr. Barnes is our man. He was the last person to be seen with her."

Sam shook her head. "I've seen this guy in action at the club. Everyone there has. Why would he kill the very girls he'd been seen with? Mr. X has been smart for years. This would be out of character."

"It's my call. I say this is our guy. A jury will just have to prove otherwise."

"You've been wrong before."

Hastings glared at her. "This is my call."

Vincent heard enough. He closed out his live show and focused on the Hungarians. Hours later, he still came up empty. The only thing he knew for sure was that Dr. Barnes was not Mr. X and Sebestyen can't keep his hands off the girls.

He rubbed his temples. What did Dr. Barnes do to catch Mr. X's attention? He's doesn't have a rap sheet for an easy fall like Mitchell Harold, but yet he's being set up. Mr. X was playing them again. Everything in his gut told him so.

Chapter 15

Vincent rang the bell to Stacy's house. Just because the police felt they had their guy, it wouldn't stop him from investigating. Prior to leaving Sebestyen the night before, Vincent left a tracker on the man's car. Now he no longer had to follow him. He'd know his every move.

The woman answered, thankfully wearing clothing instead of an open rob. She looked him over and smile spread across her face.

"Do I know you honey?" She licked her lips slowly, sizing him up as her tongue slid across the gloss.

Vincent was immune to her attempt at seduction. "No, but I'd like to have a word with you."

She crossed her arms. "What about?"

"This guy." He held up a photo of Sebestyen.

"Really?" she huffed. "Look I'm a stripper not a prostitute. I'm not going back there. I don't care how fine you are. I'm not sleeping with you or sucking your dick for no amount of money."

"Whoa, calm down. I'm not here to make you do anything. I just want to know about this guy."

"He's an asshole." She cocked her head.

"Can you be more specific? Has he hurt you?"

"No. He's ruffed up some other girls who quit though. If he come acting crazy again I have something for him. He'll get to meet Hello Kitty." Her beauty faded behind the tough girl act.

Vincent raised a brow. "Hello Kitty?"

She adjusted her arm to the side of the door out his view. What she came back with made Vincent take a step back. A pink .22 millimeter pistol with a white cat on the handle lay in her hands. "Here she is."

"Got it." Vincent heard and saw enough. "Thank you for your time."

He walked back to his car. If Sebestyen roughed up a few of the girls would he do as much as torture and murder them if he didn't get his way? The ego was a powerful thing. Domestic violence cases popped in his head. The ones in which the male ended up killing his other half for no longer wanting to be with him. Sebestyen may be suffering a form of it. If he can't make money off the girls then no one would. The ultimate control.

His tablet flashed, pulling him from his thoughts. There was movement from Sebestyen. He'd finally woken up and was on the move again. His first stop, a local Hungarian diner.

Vincent decided to get himself something to eat as well. But, the food never got a chance to reach his mouth. The tracker was on the move again. This time a location he knew. It was rental property address provided on Sam's application.

He slapped a twenty on the table and ran out of the small eatery and to his car. Once inside he revved up the engine and floored it the few blocks to the house.

Sebestyen crossed in front of his car, making direct eye contact with Vincent as he walked back to his vehicle. Vincent waited until Sebestyen pulled off before exiting his car.

What the hell where you doing here? He went up to the door and walked around checking the windows. Nothing was out of place and no signs of someone trying to gain entry that didn't belong.

Vincent frowned and turned towards his car. The flag in the upright position on the mailbox caught his eye. He opened it to find a brown envelope.

His phone vibrated, catching him off guard. He'd been in a zone all day. Seeing Sam's name on the display made him smile.

"Hey," he answered.

"Hi. I just wanted to check in with you. I'm on my way out of town."

"Taking advantage of your time off?" He walked back to his car.

"Yes. I'm going to see my parents."

He tore open the end of the envelope and shook his head. Money. "Okay. Be safe. I have something for you when you get back."

"Thanks. I'll talk to you later."

The call ended.

Vincent resumed his surveillance of Sebestyen. Every location brought him no closer to answers. Following Sebestyen proved no better than a dog trying to catch its own tail.

Day four of playing eye spy and still nothing. Outside of discovering Sebestyen had a serious drinking problem, loved money and a bad temper Vincent was still at square one. If he were guilty then so was half the city.

He whipped his car into the parking lot of Pleasures and prepared for another evening of work. The place seemed different now that Sam no longer walked through the doors. He went about his routine as a mindless robot, eagerly waiting until his shift ended in order to get back on the case.

While in the security office he kept tabs of Sebestyen on his tablet. Just like the other three days his suspect followed the same routine. He stopped by the diner, his brothers, dropped off money and then to the private party. After the party he always had to have someone drive him home because he was too drunk. In between the shenanigans he'd stop by a dancer or two's house and harass them but not much else.

Vincent came to the conclusion that this wasn't the guy either. Just to be sure though, he'd keep his eyes on him for another night or two.

Chapter 16

Sam needed to get ready for her shift but nothing felt right. Getting into it with her sister the day before didn't make things better either. Sam showed up at her parent's house the day after her father's party.

"Oh, now, you want to waltz in?" Tracey's eyes cut into her.

Sam ignored her and went straight for a hug from the frail man sitting in his favorite rocking chair. "Hi, Pop."

"Hey, baby." He kissed her cheek. Her mom stood by the door and had already given her hug upon Sam's entrance.

"How are you doing?"

"You'd know if you were here more," Tracey spat.

"Hush, girl." Their dad's tone sounded way stronger than his physical appearance. He cast Tracey a cold stare, and she ran from the room. He gazed back at Sam. His brown eyes had turned a lighter shade with age. "I'm fine. Tell me about you."

For the next hour, she talked to her dad about the case. His eyes lit up with excitement after hearing she'd been undercover. If not for a farming injury as a child, he, too, would have joined the force.

Sam only had the day off so she cut the visit short. It hurt her to have to leave so soon. She'd make it a point to come back on her next consecutive days off.

His last words to her were, "Don't worry about me. It's God's will. I've lived a great life. Now enjoy yours."

Tracey tore into her as soon as she stepped onto the porch. "You think you can just come by and all in the world is okay? Well, you know what? It's not!"

"Tracey, I…"

"I don't want to hear it. I'm the one here every day, and all he cares about is you. How proud he is and on and on."

Her words cut through Sam. "This isn't a competition."

"Isn't it? I've always been the smart one, but I'm always overshadowed by the athletic and courageous Samantha."

"Dad has always been proud of you."

"When? Did you know that he skipped my graduation for my Masters for your graduation from the academy?"

Sam's couldn't take much more of this. "Really, Tracey? Mom went for you and Dad for me. Don't you think I would have loved for Mom to be there just like you wanted Dad? Get over yourself. You chose to stay here. I didn't. Dad being sick isn't my fault."

Tears welled up in both of their eyes. Seeing their dad so sick hurt them both. The strong man they've been used to seeing had been reduced to an almost skeletal state.

"He misses you so much," Tracey's voice came out raspy. "I miss you too."

The words stopped Sam in her tracks. Tracey never seemed to like her let alone miss her. Sam rushed to her and gave her the tightest hug she could before Tracey could take the words back.

"I have to go." Sam turned and headed for her car.

The more distance she put between them the better. Her thoughts went back to the case as she drove home that night. She tried her best to protest, but it fell on deaf ears. All the higher ups were just happy to have someone. Unless Sam wanted to get reprimanded, she was advised to let Hastings handle it from there.

Sam tugged at her attire, and her mind focused back on the here and now. Being back in uniform took a bit of adjusting. She'd forgotten the weight of everything on her belt.

Sam slammed her locker. Days had passed since the arraignment of Dr. Barnes. Hastings got his way, and the Prosecutor's Office ate it up. Dr. Barnes condemned himself for his sexual misconduct of being involved with call girls.

From what Vincent said, all the girls from Pleasures who were involved in the private parties had been fired as well. Erica had one rule, and they'd all broken it. Sam didn't pity them either. Their greed overshadowed their senses. Making three to five thousand a week wasn't anything to overlook. The ten thousand she added to her bank account for a little less than two weeks of work said it all. She'd also received another five just like Skylar said, but Sam couldn't bring herself to keep it. She donated it to a women's shelter.

"Johnson says you were something to see at the club." Sam turned to see Maxis opening up her own locker. "I would have paid to see you looking feminine."

"I bet." Sam attached her cuffs to the belt and started to walk away.

"Seriously." Maxis stopped her. "That took a lot of balls. I know I couldn't have pulled it off."

"Thanks." Sam continued on. She knew it took a lot for the compliment to come out and wouldn't rub in Maxis' face. It would only be a matter of days before the niceties wore of and the insults returned. Sam would rather not start her first day back throwing jabs.

The day was just getting started, and Sam was ready to get back to her patrol. She couldn't take more of the desk work nor the compliments for a job well done she'd gotten from her peers. They could go back to only speaking when necessary for all she cared. That is, outside of the captain. He wanted her to put in for detective ASAP.

She'd think about it. In the meantime, she had drug dealers, thieves, and addicts to lock up. Sam rolled her Charger to a stop in front of the corner store.

"Long time no see, Officer Walker." Ameyn gave her a toothy grin from behind the thick bulletproof glass.

"Hey." Sam waved and walked to the cooler for her Mountain Dew. She picked up the green bottle and then set it back down. It had been weeks since she'd had one. She closed the door, moved to the next, and grabbed a Gatorade instead. Maybe it was time for a change.

Against the store owner's protests, she paid and continues outside. Just as she got ready to get in her car, movement adjacent to the store caught her eye.

Are they that freaking stupid? A drug exchange right in front of me?

The cycle never ended. Whenever one dealer was arrested, a new one would take his place. The guy in the dreads, performing the transaction, made eye contact with her and broke off down the street. Sam took off after him and bypassed the small-time buyers.

Down the alley they went. Desperate to get away from Sam, the guy yanked on the back door of a Caribbean restaurant. He must didn't get the memo that doors only remained unlocked in the movies—otherwise they risked being robbed. Dreads tried to run again, but Sam lunged. He landed face first on the pavement with Sam on his back.

He didn't bother with a struggle. Good thing too. The broken glass from discarded bottles scattered about probably would have cut deeper into his skin.

She clicked on her radio. "Dispatch, this is Walker. I have one male for transport."

"Copy that. The truck is only a few blocks away from your location," the dispatcher came back.

"Get up." Sam snatched Dreads to his feet and walked him back to the curb opposite of the corner store.

The drug dealer crew had been replaced by bystanders.

"Yo! You see those cuts on dude's face? That's police brutality for sure." A teen ran up with a cell phone and held it up to Dreads. "Don't worry, man, I have it documented."

"Move." Sam shoed him away and pushed Dreads down to the curb. "Don't get too comfy. The wagon will be here for you, and then you can ride around all night with the rest of your buddies until they take you to lock up."

"Whatever." He spat.

Before she gave him another smart remark, her cell vibrated. Seeing Vincent's name flash on the display made her smile. "Hey," she answered. Memories of their late night romp riddled her mind.

"You have a moment?" His voice came out strained.

She glanced down at Dreads. His head was slumped to the ground. He wasn't going anywhere. "Sure."

"I'm about to send you something." He ended the call.

Seconds later, a video file came through. She clicked it and immediately felt sick.

———

Vincent slowed the video down and played it again. He sat on a stool in his home and searched the background of the room for signs of anything. All to be seen were a wall with chipped paint and a crate on the ground. The woman on the screen widened her eyes with terror. Duct tape with the black letter X covered her mouth. It played for a second. Then the handwritten message covered the screen: "Causalities of war for getting the wrong guy…again. Mr. X" The words blocked his view of the scene.

This was the same video he'd sent to Sam. The video had been FedEx'd to the precinct and delivered to Hastings. The moment he uploaded the memory chip in his computer, the White Rabbit had it as well. Skylar had become the latest victim, but for now, she appeared to be alive. Mr. X was toying with Hastings.

Vincent glanced at the live feed. The captain continued chewing out Hastings as he had been for the past fifteen minutes. He pulled up a collage of all the crime scenes. *Where are you?*

He leaned back in his chair and ran his fingers through his hair. Everything was right in front of him. Vincent simply needed to figure out the message.

The ringing of his phone interrupted his thought process.

"Hey, Sam," he answered.

"The station is in a tizzy. I'm on my way back in. I assume it has to do with the video you sent me." Even her serious tone played with his senses. Another time, he'd have wished she would be on her way to crawl up in his bed.

"You're correct. The captain isn't happy, and he shouldn't be." His eyes never left the display of photos.

"Are you okay?" Sam's tone softened, and her concern filtered through the line.

"Why wouldn't I be?"

"This person killed your mother, and they locked up the wrong person…again." She let out a sigh.

As if he needed a reminder. For months after the last time, he chased after leads to nowhere. He gave up after resembling a hamster on a wheel. The closer he appeared to get, the further he was from finding the real person. Mr. X had vanished without a trail.

"I'm fine. Don't worry about me." Mr. X was the one who needed to worry. Vincent wouldn't give up this time. There'd be no threats on his job, no other cases in the way, and no reason to stop. Vincent Hunter would remain on the hunt no matter how long it took.

Chapter 17

Sam burst through the station doors and ran down the hall. The captain all but cursed her out when he called her cell. Making him wait any longer wasn't on her to-do list.

She walked right through the open door of his office and ignored Hastings, who looked like he'd been hired as the local whipping boy.

"Captain, I got here as fast as I could. What's going on?" At this point, it was best to play along. The captain would surely blow a gasket if he knew she'd gotten prior information from someone no longer associated with the department.

He rose out of his chair, towering over her and Hastings. "The problem is a detective's mess up has caused this precinct a lot of headache. I can only imagine what tomorrow's headline will read. If that freaking psycho mailed a copy of a video here, you better believe one went to the press…or, worse, bloggers. In minutes, we won't just be the laughing stock of Atlanta but the entire country."

Sam remained silent and avoided eye contact. She'd never experienced the captain this upset. The father figure version of him faded away, and Sam had no intentions on being the next victim of the shark attack.

He jammed his finger into the touchpad keyboard of his tablet and passed it to her. Once again, Skylar's face appeared, but Sam was able to handle it better. Black mascara streamed tears stained her face. The fear in the girl's eyes was almost unbearable. The video ended with the note on display.

"Do you know who this girl is?" the captain asked.

"Yes, I met her at the club. She goes by Skylar."

"No, I mean who she really is?" He leaned back on his desk. The sturdy wood held its position even though Sam could envision the captain's massive frame fueled by his heated disposition would thrust it against the back wall.

She gave him a blank stare.

"That's Darren Ivan's daughter. He's the CEO of Coca Cola and worth millions."

"Why in the world is she working at a strip club?" *And selling her body?* The information was shocking to say the least.

"Daddy issues. Who knows? She's not the product of Darren's and his wife's union."

"I see." She nodded.

"Sam, this is all yours now. The FBI will be taking over if this isn't solved in forty-eight hours." He directed his next words at Hastings. "You follow Walker's lead. I've had enough of your screw ups."

Sam swallowed hard and slowly let out a breath. She'd been dumped in the ocean without a life raft. No doubt, the FBI was stepping in because of the high profile status and not because of a bunch of dead entertainers. "Yes, sir."

"Excuse us, Hastings." The captain waited.

Hastings' head slumped, and he darted off.

"You said you didn't take the doctor for this. Do you have any ideas on who?"

Sam debated on how much she should indulge to the captain. "I think it may be someone after this Hungarian guy who often has private parties after hours."

His eyebrows lifted, softening his scowl a bit. "Do tell."

She chose her words carefully. If the captain already knew she'd been to the private party, then he'd lose it for sure. No need to pour gasoline on an already raging fire. She wouldn't lie but instead dance around the truth. "I wanted to bring it up when I had hard evidence." That part was true.

"Well, then…get on it. I'm counting on you." He gave her a pat on the shoulder.

Sam grimaced on the inside. This wasn't being sent into a game to make the final score to win the championship game. A girl's life, someone she'd gotten to know, is on the line. Not to mention all the ones before her. Going back to the party would be her only option. With Skylar missing, she could easily surmise that the guy working the door wouldn't turn her away.

"I'll do my best."

After being dismissed, Sam quickstepped back down the hall toward the front door.

"Where're you going?" Hastings was on her heels.

"To check up on a lead."

"I'm coming with you." He held open the door for her.

She didn't have time to deal with his hurt ego from screwing up. "Not unless you plan on putting on a wig, wearing makeup, and dressing in lingerie to include a thong squeezed between that hairy ass of yours."

He looked flustered.

"I'll keep you in the loop." She bypassed him and stepped out the door. "Don't worry. You'd make for an ugly woman. Let us non-detectives handle this."

Sam continued to her car. By the time she buckled up, the dejected look on Hasting's face had already been forgotten. Her focus was on preparing for tonight. Maybe she'd stop by the club first. A lot of girls did on their off days. As far as they knew, she'd had a family emergency. If questions were asked, she could say she just made it back in town. She'd check with Vincent first just to be safe.

Vincent answered his phone on the first ring, silencing the ringtone starting to play in his ear. He stood outside looking over the latest crime scene. Natalie had been taken from her apartment, but she too had been dumped in an ally. Skylar had yet to turn up and he wanted to keep it that way.

While he'd been watching Sebestyen she'd been taken. If felt like a punch to the gut. He was running out of options.

"Hey, things aren't looking good for the home team. I'm back on the case," Sam said.

"I figured as much." Well, really he'd watched as much. He'd tuned out once he learned the FBI would be involved. They'd come in guns blazing in the hopes of paying off a ransom that didn't exist. That wasn't Mr. X's motive. Almost two decades of killings proved that. Keeping Skylar alive could only be a taunt.

"I think I should go visit the private party tonight, but stop by the club first. Your thoughts?"

Vincent ignored the homeless guy who stopped digging in the dumpster and asked for change. Instead, he continued analyzing the crime scene. Looking at pictures was getting him nowhere. He needed to be in the moment and examine the surroundings. "Where are you now?"

"Headed home to change clothes."

"I need you to come see me first. I'll text you the address." Vincent hung up the phone and quickly sent her the location he'd head to next.

He chided himself for not seeing it before. All the murders in Reynoldstown made an "X," just like the ones now. Mr. X wasn't just leaving his name, but he'd literally marked a spot. The previous murders left a body right in the center, and the location was a house.

Vincent made it back to his car from the ally and drove the short distance in no time. He rolled to a stop in front of a single family dilapidated home. The image brought back memories of Mitchell Harold, the first person locked up and accused of being Mr. X. The only reason the man wasn't free right now was because he'd been a typical loser. Months later, when Mr. X struck again and proved Mitchell Harold innocence, it didn't provide a release. Mitchell's armed robberies and burglaries caught up with him. His fingerprints matched other petty crimes as well. Three strikes gave him the max of twenty-five years without the possibility of parole.

Sam's car rounded the corner just as he shut his car door. She made her exit and came toward him. His heart warmed. Sam in uniform was a sexy sight.

"What's with the abandoned house?" She gave him a quick hug.

"This is where Mr. X wanted us to look the first time. The problem was it was a setup. Mitchell Harold didn't kill anyone. Through happenstance, he became the perfect fall guy."

She frowned. "So what are we doing here?"

"I hoped it would provide clues. Mr. X is marking his territory again but we need a body for the exact location. I'm trying to prevent that." He walked toward the side of the house, giving it a thorough once over. "Why Mitchell? He was a nobody."

Sam followed close by. "Did anyone look into his family?"

"I did on my own. He doesn't have anyone. He was a foster kid. There was a wife, but she'd left years before his arrest. The neighbors said she'd been abused. She ended up in the hospital a few times. I can't blame her for leaving." They stopped in the back yard. Across from it sat an empty lot.

"Sounds like a real stand up guy." Her sarcasm didn't go unnoticed. "Why'd you stop? You see something?"

Vincent gazed across the overrun grass into the run over parking lot. "One of the victim's was found over there…my mother." He'd never allowed himself to see the place in person. Even seeing the picture was too much. He felt lightheaded and needed to sit down.

"Oh no. I'm sorry."

"It's fine. We're going to catch this guy." He pulled himself together and headed for his ride. "Meet me at the club around eight. Most of the guys for the private soirées stop in there first. You can sit at the bar and check them out, and then I'll get you wired up for later."

"Got it."

His head continued throbbing as he closed his door. He was so close he could feel it. Not wanting to waste time running a search himself, he went for the next best thing.

Vincent pulled out his phone. "Dial White Rabbit."

The phone rang.

"What can I do for you?" her perky voice sang into the line.

"You know that 'X' we noticed for the recent murders?" He pulled away from the house.

"Yup."

"I don't think he's leaving his signature. I think it's clue. X marks the spot."

"Like on a pirate's map?"

"Exactly. We don't have a body for the exact location yet, but we can narrow it down to at least a mile. Do me a favor and check on all the properties within a mile radius of the center in all directions."

"On it."

He hung up and headed for home. Vincent needed to try and relax before this evening. It would be a long night.

Chapter 18

If that guy groped Sam again, she'd throw up. His putrid breath bruised the length of her neck as he breathed along it.

"I saw you before." A thick accent accompanied his words. "Someone else took the chance before I had it."

She clinched her fists and released them, and the urge to slam him to the ground like her instincts demanded subsided. Mr. X was there, she felt it. The only way to catch him was by playing along. Kicking this loser's ass would alert everyone else that she didn't belong. "I guess you need to be quicker then."

"That's no way to get what you want." A man interrupted them.

Sam trained her focus on a clean cut guy, the same one who'd chatted her up at Pleasures. She smiled at the investment banker and flipped her long raven locks in his direction.

"First come first serve," Rank Breath countered.

"Ah, you forget the rules. The girls must be willing. From the look on her face, I don't think that's the case." The man stood his ground.

"Rules? Screw the rules." He grabbed Sam's arm.

A large hand rested on his, freeing his grasp on Sam. "Is there a problem, brother? *Van-e valamilyen probléma testvér?*" It was the Hungarian. In the commotion Sam didn't see him leave his chair. He turned to her. "Forgive Sebestyen. He's had more than enough drinks for the night."

"It's okay."

The Hungarian led his brother away.

"A pimp with a heart," she mumbled.

"Or looking after his own investment."

How could she be so careless and speak the words out loud? She needed to get her sarcasm in check and fast. Play the role.

"I'm Fitz. I didn't get to properly introduce myself earlier." He extended a hand. "And you?"

"Drunk." She shook her glass for emphasis. He didn't need to know it was only Sprite with a drop of alcohol. The drink was less potent than a dose of original Nyquil.

He took the glass from her. "I'd prefer for you to come with me willingly. No more for you tonight. Now, your name?"

"A regular Casanova. Except he's trying to woo someone he thinks sells her body," Vincent came through the earpiece.

Sam coughed to keep from laughing. "Mystic."

"I want your real name, not the stage name."

"You're getting a bit personal, aren't you?" What difference did having her name make? They weren't speaking with the hopes of going a date. She half listened to his comeback as she kept an eye out on the room.

The Hungarian went back to lounging in his chair while his brother sulked in the seat next to him. Laughter escaped the lips of girls as they held the hand of random men and led them up the stairs. A gentleman stood off in the back of the room, shifting from one foot to another. His body language was off. He avoided the girls and seemed aloof. Also, his attire appeared more thrift store than high end.

He noticed Sam glancing in his direction and immediately turned his head.

"I know this isn't the optimal place, but I saw you at the club in regular clothes and thought you were kind of nice…" the man next to her continued speaking.

"Excuse me a moment." Sam grabbed her drink off the table and seductively walked over to the evasive man in the corner. "Hi." She gave him the sexist smile she could muster.

Little beads of sweat formed around his brow. The outdated glasses he wore stood out, too big for his small face. "I'm not interested." He pushed his untamed hair out his face and she noticed how much younger he was than the other men in the room.

She inched herself into his personal space. "Sure, you are or you wouldn't be here."

He crossed his arms and backed up. "No, I'm not. If you'll excuse me." He brushed passed her.

"Did you get that?" she whispered to Vincent.

No response.

"Vince?"

What the heck was this idiot up too? He'd blow the whole thing. Vincent made a quick exit from his van and ran down the block.

An arm went up to knock on the door.

"I wouldn't do that if I were you." Vincent stopped Hastings in his tracks.

The scowl given wasn't hard to discern as Hastings walked back down the stairs. "What the hell are you doing here?"

"I could ask the same of you, but we need to move before the door opens and a couple walks out. I'd hate for anyone to recognize you. After all, you've been on the TV all week." Vincent took a step in the direction away from the house. Hastings had no choice but to follow.

Hastings shoved his hands in his pockets. "I followed Sam here. When we spoke earlier, I thought she only planed on going to the club. She had no business coming here alone."

"She didn't." Vincent led them across the street to his van. He taped the back, and the door swung open with the help of the White Rabbit.

"Who?" Hastings' mouth dropped.

"Get in." Vincent gave him a helpful shove.

Once they were both inside, she closed the door.

"You better hope no one saw us." Vincent huffed and posted back up in his seat.

"They didn't. Well, not unless they were looking out a window. I doubt if anyone from the freak house did though. I'm sure they're way too busy looking at other things." She pecked away on her computer, not giving Hastings the courtesy of a hello.

"What are you guys doing?" He glanced at the laptops the White Rabbit used and the monitors mounted to the inside of the van running a live feed on the inside of the house via Sam's hidden camera.

"Providing support. Which you almost ruined. What the hell do you think they would have done if a cop showed up at the door?" Vincent chided.

"I had no idea what was going on inside there." His eyes didn't move from the cameras.

"And that's exactly why you should have stayed put. Sam's a big girl. She's not walking into anything blind."

"This is coming from a guy who couldn't hack it as a detective."

Vincent expected nothing less from Hastings. Shoot low blows to take away from his own failings had always been his motto.

He leaned in close, ensuring Hastings understood each syllable to follow. "What I couldn't hack were the inadequacies of the department, mainly you, to solve murders. I see I was right as you've repeated the same offense again."

Hastings face went bleak but only for a moment. "I was under so much pressure to catch him. All leads pointed his way."

Vincent tried biting back his next words, but they came out anyway. "Except Sam empathically telling you that you had the wrong man."

The bravado slipped further away. Hastings sighed, studying Vincent a moment, and then, as if there was something pumping him full of life again, he came back with, “How the hell would you know what she did? Are you sleeping with her?”

The clacking of the keyboard ceased. White Rabbit’s eyes peered over the edge of her laptop and rotated from Hastings to Vincent.

Hastings stood there, eager to pounce no doubt, ready to fight for a woman he’d discarded like something as useless as a penny with a hole in it.

Vincent remained calm. A childish outburst would not make him forget his mission. Unlike the man before him, failure wasn’t an option. His attention returned to the monitor. The number of men left in the room with Sam had dwindled down to a slim few. She’d either have to go up to a room with one or leave with one if she didn’t get out of there soon.

His attitude back in check he addressed Hastings. “Whatever happens or doesn’t happen is between me and my long term friend is none of your concern. However, we’ve discussed many things being that I’ve been helping her with the case.”

The expression on his face couldn’t quit be discerned. Hastings must have realized how silly he looked and sat down instead of trying to stand and risking bashing his head against the roof of the van.

Moments passed. The clacking of the keyboard resumed, and Vincent’s trained eyes focused on Sam.

He clicked the earpiece. “Sam, we have way more than enough footage. Make up an excuse and leave.” This wasn’t working. I new idea came to him. With Hastings help they could cover the men once they left the parties. It would be easier now that he knew the same ones frequented the house. Tomorrow would be a better try. Heads would be cooler and they can go at it with a game plan.

Sam grabbed her jacket from off the back of the chair. “I’m not feeling too well. I think I’ll head home.” The gentleman she spoke to face dropped. He was dejected. “When I return, I’ll be sure to look for you.”

His eyes lit up again. He gave her a nod and adjusted his attention elsewhere.

She maneuvered through the room and neared the door.

“I’ll walk you out.”

Vincent could hear the man but not see him. He willed her to turn around and face him. Slowly, the guy with the glasses came into view.

“No thank you. I’m fine.” She politely bowed out.

“Please, I insist,” He said, his tone more of a plea than really wanting to provide chivalry.

“Fine.”

Vincent addressed Hastings, “Trail that guy.”

Hastings opened his mouth to protest.

“One of us needs to. I’m already linked with Sam.”

White Rabbit flung the door open for emphasis, and a hunched over Hastings made his exit. She quickly pulled the door shut behind him. “Such a charmer.”

The front door to the house pulled open, and out stepped Sam. She brushed the strands of hair assaulted by the wind out her face. On her tail came the man with the glasses.

“Are you following?” White Rabbit asked as she clicked off the monitors.

“Of course.”

"Then this is where I make my exit too. Do me a favor and talk about more than work. I can tell you like her." She closed the laptop and put it in her bag.

"Hold on. I'm not letting you walk around this area alone." He ignored the other part of her statement.

She smiled at him. "Such the father figure. No worries. A friend is waiting down the street. We have a serious hack competition going on, and he's been patiently waiting." The White Rabbit opened the door and disappeared into the darkness after gently closing it.

"Thank you so much," Sam's drained voice came through the earpiece. Her car door closed, and locks clicked in the background. "Sheesh, that guy was weird. Make sure you check him out."

"I'm already on it. Let's get out of here." Vincent started his engine.

"The best words I've heard all night."

He waited for her car to pass his and get down the block before pulling out and following behind.

"So, Vincent when are we going to go out on a real date?"

If she were in the passenger seat, she'd see the shocked look on his face. He'd seen her so much that the idea hadn't occurred to him. That, plus the fact that he couldn't recall the last time he'd taken anyone out. Work always had a way of taking up all his time. "Where would you like to go?"

"Dinner of course. Maybe a movie before or after. Don't worry. I'm not into chick flicks." She laughed.

"Somehow, I didn't take you as the type." He slowed his pace, allowing a car to pull in front of him. It was only a group of college kids, no doubt leaving one of the local bars that had just closed for the night. Still his mind wouldn't be at ease until they turned and were no longer behind Sam.

"What is it you like to do in your spare time?" she asked through a stifled yawn.

Wow. Was there such a thing? His mind flipped like a rolodex, trying to pull out anything that didn't have to do with looking at old cases, running background checks on people… He had it. "I love staying up on the latest technology."

"That will explain all the gadgets in your condo. You keep it up and I'm going to start calling you Inspector Gadget."

Sam just didn't know how close the analogy was. Outside of a dog, White Rabbit could be as close as Penny, Gadget's sidekick, as one could get.

Two more blocks and they'd be in front of her apartment. The other car finally turned, and with no other cars in the way, he saw the back of her car clearly.

"You didn't answer my question," she said matter-of-factly.

"What was that?" He pulled in a spot diagonal from her place while Sam navigated through her parking garage.

"When are we having our first date?" Her keys clanked together, signaling she was using them to get inside the building.

He'd love for her to be next to him at that moment. "Maybe after the case."

"Sounds great to me. I'm walking in now. I'll talk to you tomorrow."

"Night."

He clicked of the headpiece.

He should have had her come to his place.

As bad as he wanted her to come over, the case was starting to consume him and he wouldn't be great company, unless he was allowed to work out his frustrations between her thighs.

Their headset connection broken, he decided to call her phone. Straight to voicemail.

"Oh, what the hell. I'm here now. Screw it." He turned off the car and yanked the keys out the ignition. The chill in the air of summer relenting to fall nipped away at his bare arms as he crossed the street.

The door made a beep as he passed through, signaling a guest. The night security didn't budge from his slumber. Vincent frowned. Companies needed to start paying better if they wanted reliable help. The elevators doors opened with no wait and he stepped on.

He reached her floor in no time. When he stepped off, he realized that maybe it wasn't such a good idea to come up announced. He decided to call her again. If she said yes, all he had to do was knock.

Vincent's breath caught in his throat. Sam's door lay wide open, and her phone was scattered to pieces in the entrance.

Moments before…

Mr. X patiently waited in the darkness. The keys jiggled inside the lock. This one didn't bring the nerd boy home with her as expected, but no matter. That just made capturing her all the more easier. A rag to the face and down she went. An arm reached out to catch her before smacking the ground. No need for damaged goods. At least not yet.

It was very sweet of the security guard from the club to follow this one home for safety. Too bad he hadn't been smart enough to walk her inside. Not that it would have mattered. If it hadn't been for that attention-grabbing Detective Hastings bumbling about and almost knocking on the door, the van may not have been spotted. At least he'd been good for something.

The girl put up no resistance. Who could with chloroform? Mr. X dragged her down the hall to a waiting plastic garbage bin for transport. He made special care not to let her heels scrap along the cement floor. Mr. X shoved her in the cart, closed the lid, and rolled her right out the maintenance elevator.

With a vehicle strategically placed out of the apartment complex's camera view, it was easy to roll the cart to the trunk. Mr. X opened it and, with an inverted lift, dumped the passenger inside. He studied her and uncrumpled her body. A shoe was missing. Without the heels, the masterpiece wouldn't be complete.

A gloved hand snatched the discarded shoe out the hallway as the elevator doors dinged. Mr. X rushed down the hall and to the maintenance elevator. Vincent Hunter almost ruined the plans by deciding to come up at that precise moment.

Chapter 19

Vincent ran through Sam's apartment, searching and calling out for her. No answer. He rushed down the hall. The maintenance door is closed and locked. He runs back by the main elevator and pushed open the stairwell door. He listened, his eyes trained downward for movement.

"Sam!" His voice echoed around the concrete treads.

He whipped out his cell. Mashing nine one one, he waited.

"911, what's your emergency?"

"This is former Detective Vincent Hunter. There's being a home invasion, and Officer Walker has been kidnapped. I repeat, Office Walker has been kidnapped. I'm at 1925 Monroe…The Gables…fifth floor."

"Detective Hunter, I'm sending all available units. Do you have any description of the suspect or vehicle?" The clacking of fingers on the keyboard and other dispatchers taking calls filtered through the line.

"No. Advise officers to stop all males driving vehicles in the vicinity." Vincent clinched his fist. He should have just walked her up. Dammit, the first time he didn't listen to his gut in a long time. He punched her door.

"Detective Hunter, are you okay? I heard a long bang."

"I'm fine."

"Would you like me to stay on the line?"

"No." What the hell could she do?

"Patrols are in route."

"Thanks."

He dialed White Rabbit next.

As he thought, she answered sounding wide awake. "What can I do—"

"I need the surveillance videos for 1925 Monroe." The words rushed out as his heart rate elevated and the beating pounded against his ears.

"Hunter, what's wrong?"

"It's Sam. Mr. X has her."

"What? Never mind, I'm on it. Do whatever you can to get her back!" she screamed. "Get her back, Hunter!"

Her shrill voice tore at his core. Vincent pressed end. He dreaded making the next call, but it had to be done.

"Hastings," a groggy voice answered.

"You need to get to The Gables fast."

"Sam's place?" No judgment or teasing, just a question.

"She's gone. Mr. X."

"What the hell? I thought you were keeping an eye on her."

This wasn't the time for egos. Vincent staggered under the pressure of losing Sam. "Just get here."

The phone went dead. Vincent stepped inside her apartment. He slumped down on the wall, staring at the shattered phone pieces. This had to mean they'd gotten close, too close.

Footsteps ran down the hall. "Hunter!" a male voice called.

"In here."

Johnson stepped into the open door. "I was only a few blocks away. What happened?"

Vincent dropped his head. "I had eyes on her until she made it home. I messed up."

Johnson's blue eyes bore into the top of Vincent's head. "You made sure she got home. This isn't your fault." He moved about the room.

"I don't think she made it passed the entrance. The door was open, and nothing seemed to be out of place." Though, it was hard to tell with all the clutter about.

Within moments, almost the entire department showed up. Several stopped cars on their way in to no avail. This time of the night, there weren't many about and all who were had just left a club.

The captain stormed down the hall with Hastings hot on his heels. "Let's talk. Now." It was every bit of a command.

Vincent followed.

"Why the hell is one of ours missing?"

"Ours?" Hastings opened his fat mouth. "He's no longer on the force."

The captain glared at him. Hastings registered that this was not the right time, and his mouth slowly closed.

Vincent spoke up. "We were running a mini surveillance operation."

"We?" The captain's thick eyebrows furrowed, and he crossed his arms. "Continue." His demeanor put Vincent in the head space of being a rookie again and first walking into the captain's office fresh out the academy.

"Sir. Detective Hastings and I were both providing support to Officer Walker while she went undercover in a house known for running prostitutes out of it." He'll be nice and leave out the part of which Hastings wasn't originally involved and almost blew their cover. "Video surveillance and earpieces were used. I'll be able to provide you with those shortly."

Hastings remained mute and let Vincent tell the tale.

"On the surface, there didn't seem to be many suspects, but there was one guy. He made every effort to avoid Walker. That is, until she got ready to leave. He insisted on escorting her to her car." Vincent pulled out his phone and clicked on one of the files White Rabbit had been sending since he spoke to her last. "This guy."

"I want everything you have on this creep. Stay on him until he can't breathe unless you give him permission to do so. I'm going to have to give the media something, so make it fast." The captain walked away and left them standing there.

"You heard him. Let's go," Vincent said to Hastings.

"Where?"

"To get the other last person who saw her." Vincent stormed down the hall.

"What? I followed him. You're not putting this on me."

He stopped in his tracks. "No, but it doesn't mean the kid didn't see you and doubled back once you were off his tail."

Hastings nodded in agreement.

Sam's eyes cracked open with one of the worse headaches she'd had in her life. The blurry room spun as she tried to focus. A pungent odor sprang from the darkness, and she choked back the vomit starting to ease its way up. "Where am I?" she groaned. Hands tried to rise, followed by her head. They couldn't move. She struggled to move her arms. Restraints bore into her skin.

Piercing screams jerked her from her own dilemma. Directly across from her, light pierced the darkness. The pale illumination spilled onto a person strapped on a table angled directly back at Sam.

A slice across the abdomen opened up another wound. More screams. The woman shook against the restraints. Reality bum rushed the room and gave Sam a gut punch. Skylar? If she were there and Sam was also restrained, it mean the person about to apply the surgical tool to Skylar's abdomen again was Mr. X!

"Nooo!" Sam cried.

A masked face quickly turned in Sam's direction. "Good, you're awake." The voice was sinister, altered with a device to sound as such. "Don't worry. When I'm done with her, you're next."

Swoosh. The instrument cut through the air, slicing Skylar again. She screamed again.

Sam's body shook. Never in her life had she experienced such terror.

The blade dropped on a metal tray. Metal hitting metal pinged around the room. A hand playfully danced over the other tools, taking its time to select another item. Mr. X changed its mind, and he turned to a shelf behind them and picked up a film, x-ray film. He held it to the light above Skylar. "Someone has implants."

"Oh, God, no!" Skylar whimpered.

Sam blinked. This had to be a dream. No one was like this in real life. This wasn't happening.

Skylar cried out again.

Oh, but it was. This couldn't be where it would all end for Sam, not like this. She'd yet to tell Vincent she'd loved him from the moment she'd laid eyes on him. She wouldn't get to tell her father she was sorry for staying away for so long nor feel another gentle hug from her mother.

Sam sighed. *Get it together. Be strong.* She strained her eyes to see her surroundings. The walls had no windows. Maybe a basement?

She blocked out Skylar's cries as best she could. *Listen.* Water. People. Anything? Nothing.

Chapter 20

Vincent slammed his fist on the table. The guy from the private party trembled in his seat. His brown thick round-framed outdated glasses slipped down his face, and he pushed them up.

"Where is she?" Vincent demanded.

There was no time for good cop bad cop. Only bad cop.

Hastings pushed his finger into the man's temple. "Things are only going to get worse from here on out."

The guy leaned away but any farther and he'd fall out the chair. "I told you. I only walked the girl to the car," he whimpered.

"Did Daddy forcing you to the whore house piss you off?" Vincent asked. White Rabbit had come through with the information as usual. The quivering sack of shit was the step-son of Terence Brown, defensive tackle for the professional football team. Apparently good ole Terence couldn't handle being MVP and the boy's sexual preference for men. He paid for him to get laid by a prostitute. Terrence lived up to his bad boy image and then some. "Were you upset by a woman trying to coax you into sex that you just snapped?"

The guy burst into tears. Vincent and Hastings exchanged a look. Not at all the reaction they expected. Teen girls held up better.

"It's not our guy." Hastings shook his head.

"You think." Vincent's phone vibrated.

White Rabbit: *I found something interesting with the properties.*

"Give me a moment," he said to Hastings and stepped out of the room, cell phone in hand already dialing her number. "What do you have for me, baby girl?"

"There are four structures closest to the center of the X—a physician's clinic, high-rise condos, a strip mall, and a hotel." For once, her words weren't followed by a joke.

"Go on."

"The clinic is Dr. Barnes'. I did some more digging, and the other buildings are owned by his wife's family. It doesn't make sense because Dr. Barnes wasn't our guy."

His gaze went to the room on the other side of the glass. The boy still whimpered. Hastings paced the room. His eyes were hallowed and he looked as he'd aged overnight. Vincent closed his eyes. He'd no doubt wore the same haggard look.

Then it hit him. "Dr. Barnes wasn't our guy, but the murders started up again with a girl he'd paid for sex." Energy sparked within him. "I'll call you back." Vincent burst into the interrogation room. "Cut the kid loose."

"What?

"Just do it." He turned on his heels and almost knocked another officer over in his sprint to the captain's office.

He didn't bother with knocking. "Captain?"

The phone the captain was on lowered. He gave Vincent a nod.

"It wasn't Dr. Barnes, but definitely someone associated with him."

"How do you know?"

"All the places were the girls' bodies were found make an X. The first center point was Mitchell Harold's residence, and this one has been narrowed down to four associated with Dr. Barnes."

"And both were set up."

"Right! We need to speak with his wife as soon as possible. He has enemies, and she will know who."

"The faster we get to her, the faster we get Sam back. That other girl hasn't turned up yet so there's hope." The captain's eyes reflected otherwise, the gray in them void, betraying his words.

"Yes, we will." Vincent walked out the Captains' office and found Hastings waiting outside the door.

"What's going on?" Hastings asked.

"Come on. You drive." If Vincent was going to bring the woman in, he'd better at least have a government-issued car to do so.

Hastings led Vincent to his car and closed the door after taking a seat. "You mind telling me where we're going?"

"To pick up Mrs. Dr. Barnes for questioning."

Hastings cast him a doubtful glance. “I thought we already barked up that tree. I’m sure I’m not who that family wants to see right now.”

He had a point. “That’s why I’ll do the talking.” Vincent leaned back in the passenger seat. The wrong move could send the woman running.

The car rolled up the winding path, and a luxury mini mansion with Roman pillars in front came into view complete. Hastings navigated the circle driveway and parked in front.

Angst bubbled in the pit of Vincent’s stomach. He didn’t have time to play nice with the woman. Sam’s life was on the line.

Frown lines itched their way in the creamy face of the green-eyed woman who answered the door. “May I help you?” From her tone, she’d expected someone else.

“Mrs. Barnes?” Vincent asked.

“Yes.”

Being married to a plastic surgeon, he’d half expected to see a woman with the face of a porcelain doll, not someone who’d aged gracefully into their forties.

“Please excuse the intrusion. I’m Vincent Hunter, and I’m here on behalf of APD.”

Her eyes narrowed, and her head tilted, trying to see the person waiting in the car. Vincent adjusted to the side and blocked her view.

“On behalf? So you aren’t a detective?” she asked, her voice skeptical.

“I used to be. That’s not a concern though. I’m here under their full authority.” He slouched, making his frame less threatening.

"What do you want? I'm in the middle of something. I'd thought they'd finished dragging my husband's name through the mud." She seemed to be making a stand, not moving from the door and not inviting him in either.

"Ma'am, I'm not here to tarnish your husband's name. I'm here to hopefully help clear it."

Her lips pierced with doubt.

Change of tactics. No way she'd come down to the station willingly. He'd just have to go for it now. "We know Dr. Barnes isn't behind this, but we do think it's someone who is out to get him."

"How so?"

"Mr. X is known for leaving clues as a signature. Well, in this case, the clues are leading to property owned by your husband and you."

She stepped forward and pulled the door up behind her, ensuring whoever was on the other side couldn't hear her next words. "I've had my own doubts. Lately, things haven't been so well for his business. I'm not positive if he owes money to someone, but I do know the office was broken into a few months back. They completely trashed the place. He blamed kids, but I didn't buy it. Kids don't take medical tools."

Thoughts of his own father owing debts came to mind. "Has anyone approached you?"

Her hand flew to her chest, almost too quickly. "Me? Heavens no."

Her reaction to the question didn't sit well. Too staged. She was hiding something. "Okay. I'm sorry to have bothered you, Mrs. Barnes. Thank you for your assistance."

She nodded and escaped behind her door.

Vincent descended the stairs and back to the car.

"See, I told you she'd be no help." Hastings put the car in gear.

"Actually she was. She just wouldn't have gotten in the car with you inside." Vincent reached in his pocket and secured his cell.

"What did she say?"

"It's what she didn't." He pushed the last number dialed.

"Hey," the White Rabbit answered in a concerned voice.

"Do a hack on Dr. Barnes and his wife's bank account. I need to know if any large sums of money have gone out."

"Got 'cha." She hung up.

Hastings gave him a sideways glance. "What's up? I won't even get into how you just asked someone to commit a crime."

"Looking for a motive. I don't believe for one moment that Mrs. Barnes isn't the least bit upset about her husband's infidelity, and now she claims the business isn't doing well. Maybe she paid someone to frame him. Someone who had no problem getting back into their old habits." Mrs. Barnes didn't look the type for slumming, but maybe the man had approached her. Maybe he'd even been the one to tell her about her husband. In all his days, he never saw a woman who'd gotten cheated on go on the defense to stop the department from ruining an already tarnished name.

"Good point? Where to now?" Hastings' hands drummed the steering wheel.

"Dr. Barnes' office. We need to look in his basement as well as the other buildings." Seven hours had passed. His heart cried out for Sam. He shuddered to think of what torture she'd endure at the hands of Mr. X.

The car picked up the pace, and they sped the few blocks downtown. The car slowed in front of the plastic surgeon's office.

"How do you suggest we get in Sherlock?" Hastings asked. "No warrant."

"I don't need one." Vincent pushed numbers on his phone.

"Hey. What do you need?" the White Rabbit answered.

"A bypass on the security system for Dr. Barnes' office."

"I'll do you one better. The doors run on a key card access. Just a few moments…and…it's unlocked."

Within moments, Vincent and Hastings were in a basement surrounded by medical supplies.

"How much silicone does one man need?" Hasting pushed a box of prepackaged breast implants out the way. The box lost balance and fell. Implants burst free of the box and scattered.

"Quit messing around."

Hastings shoved the supplies back in the box.

"Hold on." Vincent stopped him from putting the box back on the shelf. "There's a door behind this shelf. Help me move this thing."

Hastings dropped the box and moved to the other end of the metal shelf. Together they carried it back a few feet. On instinct, both secured their guns. Hastings put his hand on the knob and, with a head nod from Vincent, pulled it open.

Gun first, Vincent stepped inside. Darkness only allowed for a few feet of vision. He kicked at a covered-in-dirt iron object in front of him. “I need a light.”

Hastings pulled out his flashlight and shined it on the ground. “What the hell is it?”

Abandoned railroad tracks extended in four directions, making a lower case “t.”

“The original Atlanta Underground.”

“It doesn’t look like much shopping went on down here.”

“Because it didn’t. This is part of the rail-line built in the 1920’s. The shopping came later…on the southern end. This actually was the ground level until the city built viaducts on top.” Vincent carefully examined the area.

“I don’t even want to know how you know this stuff. Why do you think the door was blocked off?”

“I’m thinking it was left up to the building owners. Over time, I think they’d been forgotten.” He wondered how close the other structures were to their position. He retrieved his phone and took a look, his eyes widening at the revelation.

Chapter 21

Sam's stomach churned, coupled with her fear. Skylar's body lay lifeless, still strapped to the table. A door creaked open and closed, and Mr. X appeared again. He stared at the body then injected her with a clear substance from a syringe.

Skylar jerked back to life, and the screams commenced.

"Tsk. Tsk. No one can hear you." Mr. X unbuttoned Skylar's blouse.

"Leave her alone, you sick bastard!" Sam screamed as best she could, her throat parched from the drugs and lack of water.

Mr. X's head snapped in her direction. "Let's see how you hold up when it's your turn. Anyone can kill someone. But having the heart to make a person truly suffer takes planning and skill."

"Screw you!"

"No, that's what got you here. Taunting married men with your body. I will take away every bit of vanity from you. When I'm done, no one will want you. Only pity you. You'll be just another dead corpse." The leather-gloved hands used a Sharpe to trace the outline of Skylar's right nipple. He set down the marker and grabbed the scalpel. "So eager to alter yourself to look like a whore. What will I find on you, Samantha?"

How does he know my name? The sick bastard had been watching her. Mutilating girls and killing was what? Some twisted vigilante stuff?

The knife dug into Skylar's skin with no anesthesia. Her screams cracked through the air. Sam struggled against the restraints again with little effect. Her body was weakening.

The knife pushed in and withdrew the implant. Rotten diaper smell permeated the room. Skylar had released her bowels. Her body lay limp again.

"I guess it's your turn."

Mr. X moved closer. Only his cold blue eyes could be seen behind the mask. A hand gripped Sam's head, yanking it to the side. He released then squeezed her breasts, one then the other. Sam jerked her body. A swift hand movement connected with her face.

Pain. The room faded out again.

"Stop moving!" Vincent commanded. "Shh!" He listened for the screams again. They were faint, but he'd definitely heard them off in a distance.

They were back where they started, searching for answers in the darkness. Silence.

"There's nothing here. We've checked the other properties." Hastings' voice was overcome with frustration.

Vincent walked to where the tracks intersected. "Light."

Hastings flashed it on the area. The beamed flicked across a rusted metal door.

"X marks the spot." Vincent sprang into action, yanking the door open.

Hastings jumped out of the way just as the metal door landed in the precise spot.

Vincent looked into the opening. A ladder led downward. Screams echoed around the crevice. Adrenaline took over. That better not be Sam. He scrambled down the stairs. Vincent was running down the hall by the time Hastings reached the bottom.

A door with a thin beam of light flickering underneath stopped him in his tracks. He willed Hastings to get down the hall. More screams. Vincent turned the knob, and they rushed in, guns at the ready.

"Drop it, you son of bitch!" Vincent yelled.

A hand swooped down intent on its target.

Bang!

His shot went into the shoulder holding the knife. Mr. X fell to the ground. Vincent rushed closer and kicked the weapon out of way. Hastings followed with cuffs. Vincent's eyes watered as he registered the horror. Sam looked lifeless. He slowly neared her.

Hastings' voice calling in the scene echoed in the background.

Vincent stopped in front of her. He'd never forgive himself if she didn't make it. Skylar was a goner. The open wounds from her torture told the tale.

Sam stirred. "Vincent? Is it really you?" Her words slurred. "Show me."

"It's me. I'm here." He tried to remain calm as he ripped at his shirt. He pressed the torn material against the slice on her left cheek.

She winced. "No…show that you'd be the kind and caring man I need you to be and that I'm not holding on to some fading memory of a fairytale."

His heart cried out to her. Hastings went to work with him and helped unleash the restraints. Her body freed, Vincent scooped her up into his arms. The words, unsure if they were drug-induced, caused his head to swim. For years, the knight in shining armor is all he'd wanted to be for her. The floor boards creaked as he carried her across the room, out the door, and ascended the ladder out of the pit of hell.

Chapter 22

Vincent stared through the two-way mirror, still unwilling to believe his eyes even though he'd seen the unmasked person at the crime scene.

Hastings repeated his question. "Why did you do it?"

"You're so cleaver. Folks like you easily overlook what was staring you in directly in the face all along. You dismissed me the first time. When poor Sarah Barnes came to me upset about her husband's spreading his crop dust around, my heart cried out to her. See, I, too, had been in the same situation with my husband Mitchell Harold." Jenna spoke candidly. She showed no signs of gloating or remorse, simply the facts for her self-serving needs. A classic sociopath. "Unlike Sarah, I wasn't weak. I fixed my problem and hers too. I got a good laugh watching you chase after the Hungarian. That idiot is all muscle and could have never pulled this off."

Hands wrapped around Vincent's waist. "That's one sick woman," Sam whispered.

He lowered his head. A bandaged covered what was sure to be a permanent scar below her left eye held together with stitches underneath. Still, she was more beautiful than any woman he'd ever known.

"I don't think any jury would have a problem convicting her. Come on. The doctor said you need rest." He led her out the door and into the main area.

"You sure you don't want your badge back?" The captain stood in the doorway to his office with a huge grin on his face.

Vincent took a good look around. "Nah."

"The door's always open." He disappeared back into his office, no doubt to continue fielding the outpour of calls he'd received from the media.

He and Sam continued out the front door.

"So what are you going to do?" Sam asked.

"Right now, take you home and make passionate love to you. Later, who knows?" He shrugged.

Sam hugged her father. He seemed healthier than the last time she saw him. This time Tracy stayed in the room with her. She too listened in while Sam recapped the case of Mr. X to their father.

Hours later her father slept peacefully.

"Are you ready to go?" Vincent stood in the doorway with her mother.

"I'm so happy for you two." Her mother gave him a kiss on the check.

"Yes. I have to get back to work. Tomorrow's my first day back." Sam hugged him. To her mom she said, "But, I promise not to stay away too long."

Her mother saw them off. Back in the car Sam enjoyed the ride as Vincent drove.

"What are you going to do with yourself now that you're no longer undercover?" he deep voice louder than the radio.

"Enjoying my life with you." She placed a diamond ringed hand on his thigh. "And, turning in my application for detective."

Vincent smiled. "I think detective suits you."

His eyes focus on the road, while her gaze stayed on him. Who knew that all those years of fawning over him would lead to this?

Vincent showed up to Pleasures at his usual time and headed straight to the boss's office.

She opened her door and welcomed him with open arms. "I have no idea how I'd ever repay you."

"No need to worry about it."

"Are you kidding me? You saved my business, and the rest of my girls are safe. You're like a hero now." She beamed.

"Thank you." He dropped his head and thought for a moment. The weight of the past tugging at his soul was no longer there. He'd repaired the void. His gaze went serious when he brought it back to Erica. "There's something I need to tell you."

"What?" She studied him. "Don't tell me." Her mouth dropped. "You're leaving."

"I have to. This isn't me. I only took the job because a part of me was missing. I found it, and now that chapter is closed."

"What are you going to do?"

"What I do best…catch bad guys." Vincent laid the keys to Pleasures on her desk and headed out. He wouldn't return to the force as the captain suggested, but he would become an asset, only on his terms—Hunter Private Investigator.

The End

****

About the Author

Ann Keeys is an Amazon best seller and award winning author in both romance and nonfiction. Her love for writing came in high school and in 2006 she penned her first novel. Since then she's had the writing bug and considers herself a multi genre author. Domestic Seduction is the first in the V. Hunter Series.

She currently resides in Atlanta with her family.

Other Books You May Enjoy

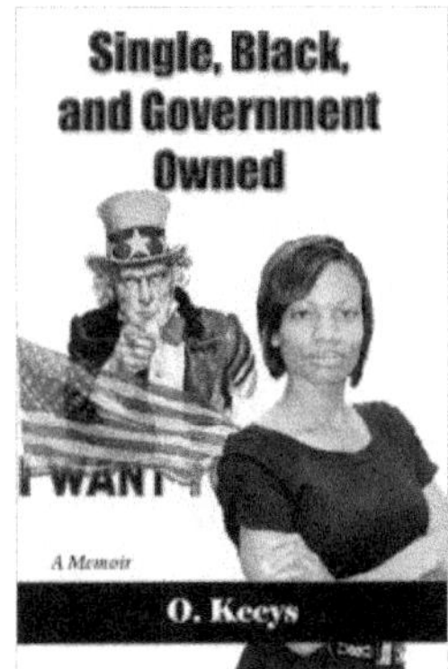

Single, Black, and Government Owned is the explosive follow up to O. Keeys's critically acclaimed memoir, *Rise and Fall of a Track Star*. After walking away from a rising track career Omegia joins the military and leaves her son at home with her family.

For nearly thirteen years she balances being a single parent, dating, and her commitment to Uncle Sam. *Single, Black, and Government Owned* is an up close and personal view into the life of a woman overcoming the challenges of being a victim of sexual assault. This memoir takes you on an emotional roller coaster ride and will leave you feeling liberated.

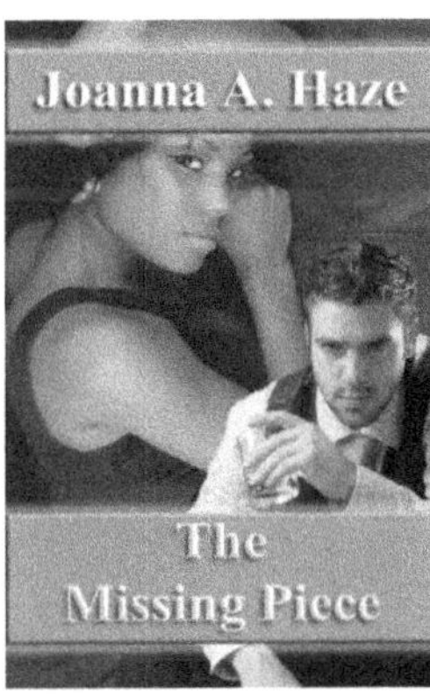

Nyla James was at her wits end. It had been three long years full of empty promises and being told the timing was not right. William not only refused to commit but Nyla had a hunch he was being less than the faithful man he portrayed.

Dean Parker has grown weary of his wife's selfishness. Susan's beautiful smile and stunning body was no longer enough to contain him. Once that wore off he began see her for the heartless person she had always been.

Once Dean lays eyes on Nyla his thoughts are instantly consumed with visions of her. Nyla is intrigued by this man of a different nationality but hesitant because Dean is someone who pulls at her inner being. Something no other man could do. Will Dean turn into another William? Or will his love be the missing piece?

www.ingramcontent.com/pod-product-compliance
Lightning Source LLC
Chambersburg PA
CBHW072126170626
46813CB00004B/1714
9780985612573